P9-CLA-925

DISCARD

WE
DREAM
OF
SPACE

ERIN ENTRADA KELLY

WE DREAM OF SPACE

 Greenwillow Books
An Imprint of HarperCollinsPublishers

This book is a work of fiction. References to real people, events, establishments, organizations, or locales are intended only to provide a sense of authenticity, and are used to advance the fictional narrative. All other characters, and all incidents and dialogue, are drawn from the author's imagination and are not to be construed as real.

We Dream of Space
Text copyright © 2020 by Erin Entrada Kelly
Schematic illustrations © 2020 by Erin Entrada Kelly; character art by Celia Krampien

All rights reserved. No part of this book may be used or reproduced in any manner whatsoever without written permission except in the case of brief quotations embodied in critical articles and reviews. Printed in the United States of America. For information address HarperCollins Children's Books, a division of HarperCollins Publishers, 195 Broadway, New York, NY 10007.
www.harpercollinschildrens.com

The text of this book is set in Bookman Old Style.
Book design by Sylvie Le Floc'h

Library of Congress Cataloging-in-Publication Data is available.
ISBN 978-0-06-274730-3 (hardback)
ISBN 978-0-06-302670-4 (int'l.pbk ed.)

20 21 22 23 24 PC/LSCH 10 9 8 7 6 5 4 3 2 1
First Edition

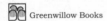 Greenwillow Books

R0458757087

"You have to dream.
We all have to dream."

—Christa McAuliffe, Mission Specialist

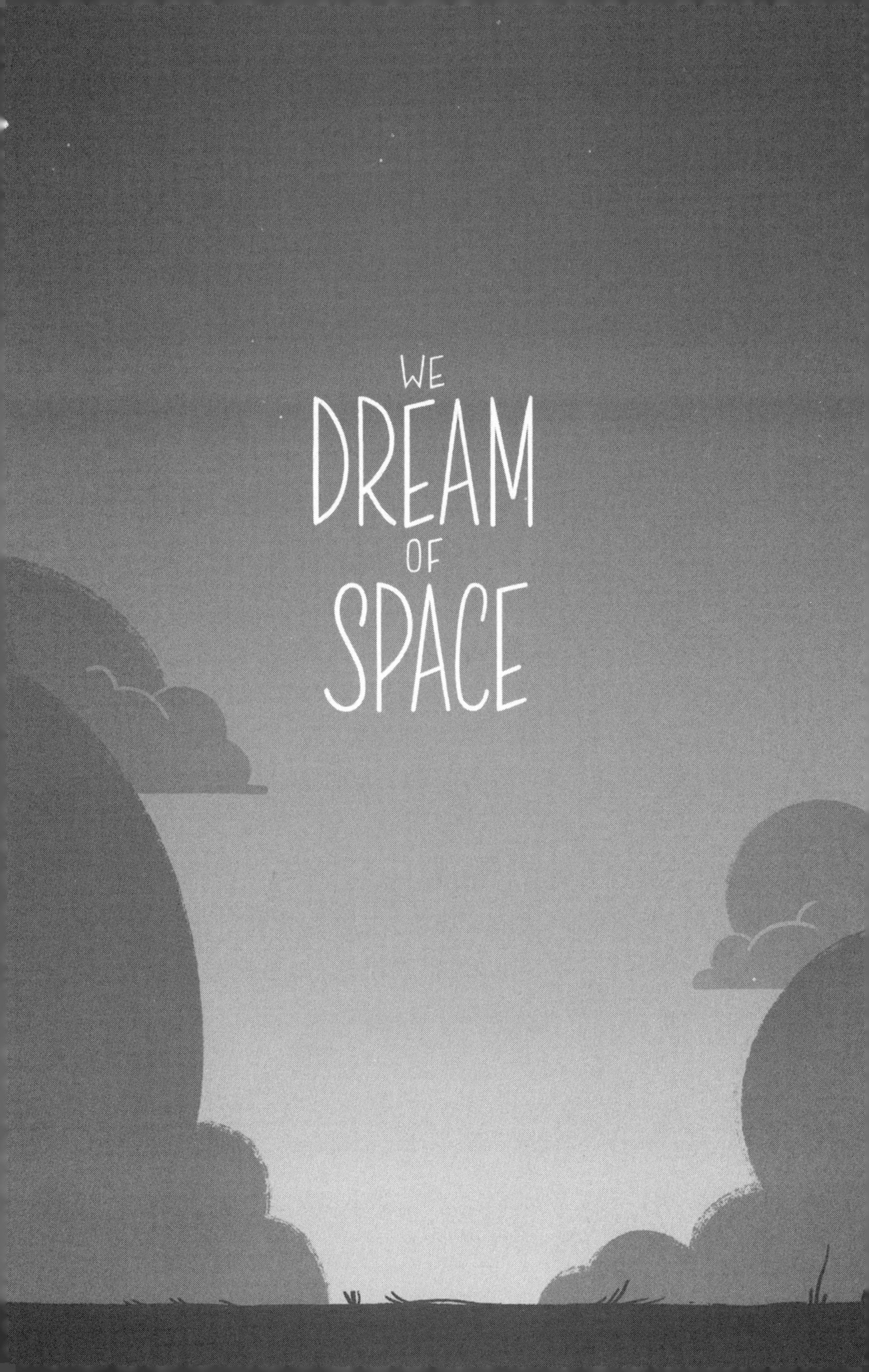
WE
DREAM
OF
SPACE

READY FOR TAKEOFF

The pinball machine didn't steal Fitch Thomas's quarter. Not really. But when one of the flippers is broken, there's no point in playing. As soon as Fitch realized this, something sparked inside him. Something ugly and familiar. He stared at the slot where he'd sunk his quarter only moments before.

Easy does it, Fitch. Just go to Mr. Hindley's office and get your quarter back. No big deal.

The blinking lights of the machine—Bright Star One, it was called—seemed out of place in the arcade today. Fitch looked around. He was one of the only people there.

Maybe it was too early for people.

It was never too early for him.

READY FOR TAKEOFF, the lights blazed. He left them behind and walked to Mr. Hindley's office.

The door with MANAGER stenciled above the frame was open, as usual. Mr. Hindley was manager, owner, and staff. When quarters were stolen, he was the man to see.

Fitch cleared his throat.

"Mr. Hindley?" he said.

Mr. Hindley looked up from his ledger. "Henry Nelson Thomas, my favorite patron! What brings you to the front office?"

This was what Mr. Hindley always said, even though no one called him Henry and Mr. Hindley's office was in the back corner of the small arcade. Nowhere near the front.

Fitch motioned half-heartedly toward pinball row.

"One of the machines is broken," he said.

Mr. Hindley placed both hands on his desk and stood up, like President Reagan ready to face the Soviets.

"That is unacceptable, patron Thomas," he said.

Mr. Hindley was what Fitch's mother would call "an odd duck," but he moved fast. Within seconds he was in front of the Major Havoc game in the center of the arcade, squinting at the screen.

"Not that one," Fitch said. He pointed at Bright Star One. "This one."

Mr. Hindley raised his eyebrows. "But you're a Major Havoc guy. One from all, all from one, fighting for humanity and all that."

Yes, it was true. On any given day, Fitch could be found at the Park, Delaware, arcade—officially named the Pinball Wizard, but known to the locals as the "arcade on Main"—playing Major Havoc, a game that his best friend, Vern Repass, said was a "*Star Wars* wannabe," even though Major Havoc had been released first, but whatever. Vern was so obsessed with *Star Wars* that Fitch had developed unfounded resentment toward Luke, Han Solo, and the whole lot of them. (Except Vader, maybe. Vader was kinda cool.) The more Vern ragged on Major Havoc, the more dedicated and defensive Fitch became, and now he was so preoccupied with beating his own high score that Major Havoc—in all his vector-graphic glory—sometimes appeared in his dreams, demanding that he get to the reactor before everyone exploded.

But today was January first, and Fitch had made a New Year's resolution to try something different. The last time he was here, his twin sister had come along and been entranced by Bright Star One, with its spaceship and lights. She didn't want to actually play it—video games were *not* her thing— but she tried to convince him to give it a chance. He'd snapped at her to leave him alone, then felt bad about it later. So he'd gone for the pinball machine this morning, even though no one played pinball anymore. And now look what had happened.

Mr. Hindley made his way to Bright Star One and tapped it affectionately.

"What's wrong with it?" he asked.

"The right flipper's broken," replied Fitch.

Mr. Hindley pushed the button. When nothing happened, he said, "It's impossible to play a respectable game of pinball with just one flipper."

Duh, Fitch thought.

Mr. Hindley disappeared into the office and emerged seconds later with a sheet of paper with "OUT OF ORDER" written across it in fat black letters. The smell of Magic Marker wafted in the air as he taped it across Bright Star One.

"Thanks for the heads-up, patron Thomas," Mr. Hindley said. He smiled. It was wide and pleasant and took up most of his face. "Anything else I can help you with?"

Yeah, you can give me my quarter, Fitch thought. But he didn't say it out loud. The fire was too bright.

THE MOOD OF A HOUSE

Ten seconds before Fitch's twin sister, Bernadette Nelson Thomas, opened her eyes, she thought: *If there's a five on the alarm clock, it will be a good day.* When the digital numbers glowed 2:32 p.m.—no fives in sight—she assumed the first day of 1986 would be a toss-up. She shouldn't have slept so late, but she'd stayed awake until four that morning assembling a new desk for her room. The job would have taken thirty minutes if she'd followed the instruction manual. But twelve-year-old Bernadette—"Bird," as she was called—was not one to follow instruction manuals. She threw it away instead, assembled the desk perfectly, then created a manual of her own. Her stack of schematics was growing, and thanks to the new desk, she now had a safe place for them.

After she forced herself out of bed, she walked quietly into the hall.

Houses had their own personalities, and Bird liked to know which one she was walking into.

She navigated around the hallway clutter—laundry baskets stuffed with clothes, short stacks of books and magazines, a box of old toys (including a Barbie that Bird had never played with, and her brothers' plastic toolbox, which she had)—and listened as she sidestepped the seemingly endless array of sneakers that littered the house like land mines. Her mother always said she would straighten up once she found a place for everything, but where would that be? They were cramped enough as it was. Her parents didn't even have their own bedroom; they'd converted the small den into their personal space. That, too, was cluttered.

Her parents were talking in low voices. That was a good sign. Bird continued into the living room, where her father, Mike, was sitting in front of the entertainment center, fiddling with buttons on the new VCR. Her mother, Tammy, was stretched on the couch with a book, saying " . . . that was the whole point of getting a new one. Or so I thought."

Bird detoured into the adjoining kitchen. She moved stained coffee mugs and random pieces of mail out of the way, then took out a bowl and spoon and placed them delicately on the kitchen counter. She stared at the cereal boxes in the pantry. She usually had Apple Jacks on Wednesdays, but maybe she should try something different. Fruity Pebbles? No, those belonged to Fitch, and he could really *pitch* a *fit*—hence his nickname—when someone messed with his things. Shredded Wheat? No way. There was a fresh box of Frosted Flakes for Cash, and he usually didn't notice if someone swiped his cereal. But Bird wasn't in a Frosted Flakes mood.

"It wasn't the *whole* point, Tam," her father said. "There are other people in this house, too."

Apple Jacks. Definitely Apple Jacks.

Bird filled her cereal bowl three-quarters full. Then, milk.

"I'm well aware there are other people in the house, *Mike*," her mother replied. "Who do you think does all their laundry after working eight hours a day?"

Bird had misjudged the house's personality. She'd been tricked once again by her parents' low voices. She'd expected Dr. Jekyll, but it was Mr. Hyde.

"Good morning!" Bird said, lifting her voice with as much enthusiasm as she could muster.

Her mother looked up from her book. *If Tomorrow Comes*, it was called. "Don't touch those sugar cereals, Bird. Those are for your brothers. You won't be skinny forever."

I wonder how many times she'll say that sentence in 1986, Bird thought. She considered counting. Maybe she could make it a New Year's resolution.

Bird returned the milk to the refrigerator. "Where is everyone?"

"Fitch is at the arcade and Cash is out with friends," Tammy said.

"I stayed up late last night putting my desk together," said Bird. She shoved a spoonful of cereal into her mouth. "It took me a while, but I got it. I even assembled the drawers and sketched a schematic of—"

"It's probably not the VCR's fault, Tam," her father said, eyes on the VCR. "You probably didn't set it right."

Her mother sighed and turned a page. "I did exactly what the instructions told me to do."

"If you did exactly what the instructions told you to do, it would have worked."

Bird carried her bowl into the living room, moved a stack of newspapers off the armchair, and sat down. Their old VCR was on the carpet, a thin coat of dust and a tangle of wires on top.

Bird had yet to disassemble a VCR. Now *that* would be a great undertaking to kick off the new year. She could remove the top of it easily with a simple screwdriver from her toolbox and take a "Bird's-eye view" of its inner workings. Study the guts of the machine.

Machines had the best guts.

"If you don't need the old VCR, can I have it?" Bird asked.

Her question disappeared just as quickly as it'd arrived.

"Your father told me this fancy new VCR would record *Days* while I'm at work," her mother said. "But today when I sat down to watch my show, the tape was totally blank. Didn't record a thing."

"What's happening with Dr. Evans these days?" Bird asked, quickly.

Marlena Evans was her mother's favorite character on *Days of Our Lives.*

"Tam, which of these scenarios is more likely?" her father said, leveling his eyes on her. He used his fingers to count off: "One, our brand-new VCR is malfunctioning for no apparent reason, or two, you didn't get the settings right?"

Tammy laid the book facedown on her lap. "Oh, you're right, *Michael*, I'm far too stupid to follow clearly written instructions for a machine as complicated as this."

"No one said you were stupid."

Bird chewed silently and focused on a speck of lint on the floor.

"I'd have to be stupid if I can't read and follow simple instructions."

"We're all well aware how smart you are. God forbid, a woman with a college degree wouldn't know how to work a VCR!"

Tammy snatched the book off her lap and sat up. "Lots of good that degree did me. I'm working as a secretary for a bunch of—"

"You're the one who insisted on going back to school and putting us in debt." Bird's father flipped through the VCR manual.

"Funny you should talk about debt when you just spent an outrageous amount of money on a gadget that doesn't even work . . . "

Bird looked into her cereal bowl and thought of Ms. Salonga, her science teacher. Before winter break, Ms. Salonga said the class would dedicate the month of January to space exploration to celebrate the launch of the *Challenger* shuttle. Ms. Salonga had taught them all kinds of facts about space—not that Bird needed to be told; she knew many of them already—but the most fascinating fact was that there was no sound in space. Not really.

Space is a vacuum, Ms. Salonga said. *If a piece of debris hits an orbiting spaceship, the astronauts inside would hear it, but someone outside wouldn't.*

As Ms. Salonga explained the process of sound and molecules, Bird snapped a picture together in her head, like a puzzle. Then she imagined her brothers and parents inside a spaceship.

And her: outside, floating. In silence.

BiRD'S-EYE VIEW:
ViDEO CASSETTE RECORDER (VCR)

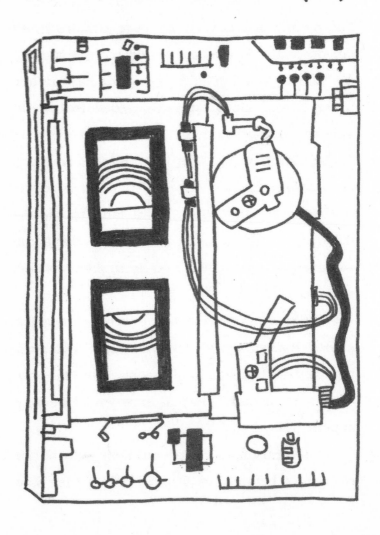

GOD OF BASKETBALL

The game was pretty stupid, to tell the truth. All you needed was a few guys and a brick wall. In this case, it was the east side of the Park Public Library, two blocks from the arcade on Main, and the guys were Cash Nelson Thomas, Justin "Brant" Brantley, and Kenny Haskins. The rules were simple: Two of them would run toward the wall, jump at the last minute, and touch the highest brick they could reach. The third guy would serve as judge to determine the victor. Thirteen-year-old Cash was quick—he used to outrun Kenny and Brant when they ran laps for Coach Farnsworth—so he usually got to the wall first. He wasn't much of a jumper, though, so he rarely won. It didn't matter, anyway. There was no prize. Only glory.

On January first, Brant and Kenny got to the parking lot before him. Typical. When they saw him appear down the street, hands stuffed in his Sixers jacket, Brant immediately called out, "No wonder you're a repeat—your butt can't get out of bed!"

"Shut up," Cash said, when he was close enough. The words came out casually but firmly, as they always did, and he swallowed a thick seed of embarrassment. As he always did.

Brant and Kenny ragged on him any chance they got for failing seventh grade, but it's not like they were geniuses. Bird could outsmart them at any turn. Kenny had barely passed last year himself.

But.

He *had* passed.

"Did you set off fireworks last night?" Brant asked. A Boston Celtics knit cap covered his curly blond hair. Cash resisted the urge to snatch it off his head. *It's not Justin's fault his parents are from Boston,* Cash's dad liked to say. All in good fun.

"We shot off a bunch of Roman candles," said Kenny. "It was awesome."

Kenny had red hair and pale skin. In elementary school, he cried because the kids called him "Carrot Head." Now all the girls thought he was handsome. He was tall, had more muscles than most of the other guys their age, and was the star of the Park Middle basketball team—a spotlight he shared with Brant. Cash had intended to be in the spotlight, too, but things hadn't quite worked out that way.

"Yeah," Cash said. "We fired a bunch."

Actually, they'd only lit a few sparklers before Fitch got mad about something and stalked to his room. Their father went in after him because their mother had fallen asleep in the armchair at eleven o'clock, still wearing her pantyhose. Then it was just Cash and Bird outside in the cold. And what did they have to talk about?

Cash and Brant took their places a set distance from the wall while Kenny hung back to keep score. No one had to announce that it was time to start. They'd been best friends since elementary school and moved like a single unit.

"You gonna watch the game tonight?" asked Brant.

"What do you think?" Cash replied. "Portland's gonna get destroyed."

"The Sixers are gonna tank after Dr. J retires," Brant said. "Enjoy it while it lasts."

Dr J.

Julius Erving.

Forward for the Philadelphia 76ers.

God of basketball.

Dr. J was the last face Cash saw before he fell asleep and the first face he saw when he woke up, thanks to a poster his dad got for him, which Cash had taped proudly to the back of his bedroom door.

"Are you guys gonna go or what?" Kenny called.

Cash took off without answering. Converse

high-tops hitting cold gravel. He jumped as high as he could when he reached the wall, but he fell short.

Just as he always did.

MAJOR HAVOC

The arcade was quiet, so Fitch was on a winning streak. Vern wasn't there to pester him. People weren't bumping his shoulder on their way to Pole Position or Star Wars. No one hovered nearby. It was just Major Havoc and him, flying a Catastrofighter through a wormhole in space so they could lead a clone army against the brainless Vaxxian robots. Fitch had just started counting his blessings when Bird burst through the doors and half jogged toward him, saying they had to go. Something about the emergency room and Cash. What was she talking about?

"Cash hurt his hand," Bird said, nearly breathless.

Fitch kept his eyes on the game. "What do you mean, he hurt his hand?"

"Just what I said. We're going to the emergency room. Come on."

"Is he dying or something?"

"No, but . . . "

"Why do I have to go, then? I'm not injured."

"His hand is swollen like a basketball!"

"Good," Fitch said. Major Havoc fell into yet another maze, tasked with touching the nuclear reactor before it exploded. He still had threes lives left. "Maybe it'll improve his one-on-one game."

"Come *on*," said Bird. "Stop playing that stupid thing and let's go!"

"You write instruction manuals in your spare time and you're calling *this* stupid?"

Someone honked. Probably his parents.

Ugh. Why couldn't he ever be left alone? He wished he could transport to another planet.

He wished he really *was* on an important space mission instead of dealing with his stupid family. He'd rather face brainwashed Vaxxians.

"Fine," Fitch said. "I'm in the middle of something, but whatever. I have *three lives left,* but *fine.*" He released the joystick and kicked the machine with the toe of his sneaker. His chest burned. It only took a second for Major Havoc to get hit. You couldn't lose a single moment. You'd get obliterated in the blink of an eye.

Bird was already back at the door when Fitch finally turned away from the game and went outside. His parents glared at him from the front seat. Fitch and Bird got in the back, where Cash cradled his injured hand. Bird was right—it was swollen. Not quite as big as a basketball, but big enough.

"What happened?" Fitch asked.

The family's Chevy Cavalier pulled out of the arcade lot onto Main Street and picked up speed heading toward New Castle County Memorial Hospital.

"I slipped on ice," Cash said, his head rested against the window, his face tight.

"Idiot."

"Hey! Language," their father said.

"At least I spend time in the real world," said Cash, without looking at his brother. "With three-dimensional friends."

"Maybe if you had a three-dimensional *brain* you wouldn't be failing seventh grade for the second time," Fitch said. "Good luck getting any homework done with your right hand in a cast. Not that you know how to do it anyway."

The heat in Fitch's chest sparked and popped. He'd had three lives left. Wasted. All because his brother was a moron.

"You're lucky my hand's broken, because otherwise I'd punch you in the face," Cash said, sliding down in his seat.

A chorus of responses rose up at once—Fitch, with a comeback; their mother, scolding; father, saying, "Hey! Language!"—but the loudest was Bird.

"I finished another issue of *Bird's-Eye View*, if anyone wants to see it when we get home," she said.

"No one wants to see your drawings," Fitch said.

The car quieted.

What kind of twelve-year-old drew diagrams for fun?

I wish I was adopted, Fitch thought.

FAMILIAR ENERGY

Everyone was exhausted by the time they got home—everyone but Bird. Partly because she'd slept into the afternoon and partly because the X-ray machine that scanned Cash's wrist had enchanted and mystified her. She'd thought she wouldn't get to see it, but she'd asked and asked, and finally her mother said yes and took her along while Fitch and Dad waited in the emergency room.

She wanted to riddle the radiation technician with a million questions, but she'd only managed to ask three before her mother told her to hush because she was "disturbing the nice young man," though as far as Bird could tell, the nice young man didn't mind answering her questions at all. When Bird asked how X-rays worked, he patiently explained about electromagnetic waves of energy. When she asked what the inside of an X-ray machine looked like, he said he wasn't sure, "but maybe something like a camera with a radiation beam." Her mom shushed her right after she'd asked how the beams were produced.

The drive home was quiet. Her father said one thing—"I wonder how the Sixers did"—but no one responded. Bird took advantage of the silence by imagining the X-ray machine disassembled in front of her. When they got home, everyone siphoned off to their respective rooms, including Bird, who spent who-knows-how-long drawing and redrawing the innards of an X-ray machine (or what she thought it looked like, at least). By the time she looked at the clock, it was 1:40 in the morning. Not good. School tomorrow.

"Tea," she said, aloud to herself.

Chamomile tea was good for sleeplessness. Ms. Salonga had told her that.

She walked quietly on the balls of her feet, trying not to wake anyone, but someone was already awake. There was a sliver of light under Cash's door.

Bird knocked lightly.

No reply.

She knocked again, turned the knob, and peeked inside.

Cash was on his bed, still dressed, even his high-tops. He was staring at the ceiling with his plastered wrist draped over his chest.

"Are you okay?" Bird stepped inside and

closed the door. Cash's room was tidy—just as tidy as hers, in fact. Nothing like Fitch's, which was an explosion of dirty clothes, soiled socks, half-read books, and Atari cartridges. Nothing like the rest of the house, with clutter tucked in every corner and stacked on every flat surface.

"I'm fine," Cash said.

"Are you going to school tomorrow?"

"I don't know. No."

"I'll ask Ms. Salonga for handouts and copies and stuff," said Bird. "And I can get homework from your other teachers, if you want."

Cash said nothing.

"Are you gonna get people to sign your cast?"

No answer. "Yeah, I guess," he finally said.

"I have a permanent marker if you need one."

A familiar energy filled the room, as if there were many things to say but no one knew what the words were. The Thomas family was like its own solar system. Planets in orbit. No, not planets. More like meteors or space junk. Floating objects that sometimes bumped or slammed into each other before breaking apart.

Time to drift back to my orbit, Bird thought.

"Thanks, Bird," Cash said, just before she left the room.

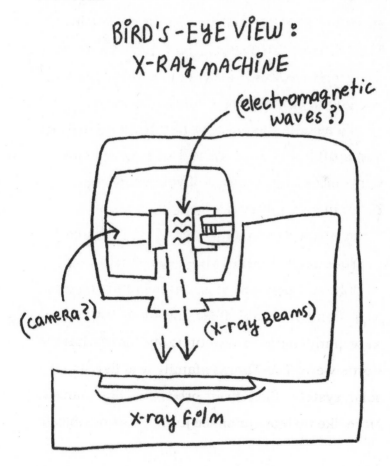

BIRD'S-EYE VIEW:
X-RAY MACHINE

(electromagnetic waves?)

(camera?)

(X-ray Beams)

x-ray film

ONE REASON

Here's what Cash wanted to say: *What's the point?*

What was the point of going to school? He was already struggling, had already flunked once, and now his hand was in a cast—the hand he needed to take notes and do homework, two things he was already no good at doing. He was okay at PE, the only subject he didn't despise (if it could be called a subject), but how would he dribble a basketball like this?

Not that it mattered.

He wasn't exactly Julius Irving.

Playing basketball was the only thing he'd liked about school. At first, anyway. He'd even kept up his GPA to stay on the team. There was just one problem: he hadn't scored a single point. It quickly became clear that he didn't add any value to the Park Warriors, not like Brant and

Kenny, who sank free throws, three-pointers, and endless jump shots. Halfway through the second season, Coach Farnsworth finally articulated what everyone had been thinking.

"You can run, but you can't shoot," he'd said. "And if you can't shoot . . . " He shrugged.

Coach didn't cut him from the team. No one ever got cut unless their grades dropped. You just got benched. Sometimes Coach put him on the court, but only if the Warriors already had a clear victory. Being dropped from the roster was a merciful end to Cash's basketball career once his grades—always on the brink of disaster—finally fell below the mark.

Coach is right, Brant had said, *Cash* can *run fast. He runs from his homework every night.* That was a favorite joke for a while.

So really. Why even go?

Well. There was *one* reason, he supposed.

Penelope Barnard. Also known as Penny.

She sat in front of him in Ms. Salonga's

WE DREAM OF SPACE

class. She said hello to him every morning—a quick "hey," like the chirp of a bird—then sat down and swept her brown hair off her neck until it dangled over the back of her chair. A waft of shampoo exploded into the air every time, and Cash wondered (every time) what scent it was.

Penny Barnard wasn't one of the popular girls, but she wasn't unpopular, either. Sometimes Cash wondered if anyone else ever noticed the way her freckles dotted her nose, or how her hair smelled, or how she smiled at everyone when she walked into a room.

And now he had a legitimate reason to talk to her.

He imagined how it would go.

Him: Hey, do you wanna sign my cast?
Her: Sure. Do you have a marker?
Him: Yep. Right here.
Her: What should I write?

Him: You can just sign your name, if you want.

Her: How did you break your wrist, anyway?

Him: I was just goofing around with the guys, and I slipped on a patch of ice.

Her (mildly alarmed): Did it hurt?

Him: Nah. I had to go to the ER and everything.

Her: That's terrible!

Him: The worst part is, I can't really take notes.

Her: I'll make a copy of my notes for you.

Etcetera.

Maybe he'd talk to her tomorrow.

Maybe he'd wait until Monday. The start of a fresh new week.

Maybe the cast would be worth something after all.

FAMILIES ARE COMPLICATED MACHINES

For a machine to work the way it's supposed to, all the parts have to do their jobs. And what is a family but a complicated machine? One loose bolt, one badly oiled gear, and the whole thing gets cranky, loud, and unpredictable. Bird prided herself on being the most reliable gear in the Nelson Thomas Family Device, so when she walked into the kitchen the next morning, she was cheerful— as cheerful as she could be at seven-thirty in the morning, anyway—but ready for anything.

Fitch was at the kitchen island, eating raw

Pop Tarts, while their parents hurriedly gathered lunch items to take to work.

"He had a long night. I don't think it would hurt to give him the day off," their father was saying.

"But his grades . . . " their mother said. She tucked a can of SlimFast into her bag.

"I told Cash I'd pick up his assignments from his teachers," Bird offered. She set her backpack on the empty seat next to Fitch and poured a glass of orange juice while her father reached around her for an apple.

"You don't even have the same teachers," said her mom.

"We both have Ms. Salonga," said Bird.

"Fitch has Ms. Salonga, too," her mother replied. She snapped her fingers in Fitch's direction. "Fitch, don't you have a bunch of classes with your brother?"

"We don't have any classes together."

"But you have some of the same teachers, correct? Not just Ms. Salonga."

"Yeah," Fitch said, his mouth full. Crumbs

tumbled onto his new Members Only jacket. He brushed them off absently. "Like, four, I think."

"Can you pick up Cash's assignments?" she said, slipping a can of Diet Tab next to the SlimFast. Tammy Nelson Thomas often lectured Bird that looks were not important, yet she seemed preoccupied with them anyway—specifically her weight, which had ticked upward over the years, and Bird's weight, which had not ticked anywhere, but apparently could skyrocket at any moment.

"I don't mind doing it," said Bird, before Fitch could complain. He was one of the squeakiest of the Nelson Thomas gears.

"That wouldn't make sense. Not when Fitch has four of the same teachers," their mother said. "Besides, you need to learn that you don't have to take care of everyone just because you're a woman."

Their father threw his head back in mock exasperation.

"Bird isn't a *woman* yet, Tam," he said. "Don't put ideas in her head."

Mrs. Thomas stopped fidgeting with her lunch bag and crossed her arms. "What ideas, exactly?"

The gears squeaked quietly, lightly.

"All these 'equal rights' ideas," he replied. "Next thing you know she'll be burning her bra in the backyard."

"I don't even have a bra," Bird said quickly, desperate to change the subject.

Fitch shoved his hands inside the sleeves of his jacket and covered his ears. "Can we *please* not talk about my sister's bra?"

Bird forged ahead: "In health class we learned that girls develop at all different rates. I may not get my period or boobs for a while."

Fitch groaned. "Make it stop. Make it stop."

Mrs. Thomas unfolded her arms, reached over the island, and pinched his arm.

"If you promise to get Cash's assignments, we promise to stop talking about bras," she said.

"I'll pick up anything you want," said Fitch. "I'll rob a bank if I have to."

"Just the assignments will do!" their mother said, smiling.

The gears quieted.

Malfunction averted.

THE NELSON THOMAS FAMILY
SCHEMATIC

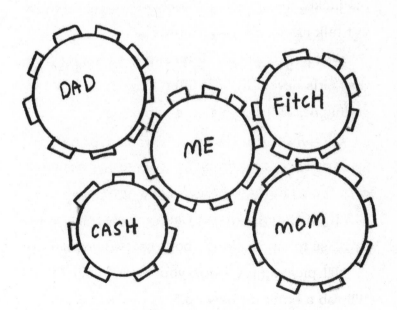

AMANDA PIPER

It all started with Darth Vader's TIE fighter. If he had never drawn the stupid ship in his stupid science notebook, nothing would have happened. But on the last day before winter break, while Ms. Salonga droned on about NASA's Teacher in Space Project, Fitch lifted his pen and drew the inverted wings and blaster cannons. He even sketched detailed panels with his ballpoint pen.

That's when he heard it. The compliment that shifted Earth on its axis.

"That's really cool."

Amanda Piper. She sat next to him. Big, curly, brown hair around a broad, round-cheeked face. A smatter of pimples. A smatter of freckles. She was taller and broader than the other girls in the class. A pinch of fat folded over her jeans. Her hands were thicker than his.

Some of the guys at school, including Vern,

had names for her. And now here she was, talking to him.

Fitch mumbled "thanks" and thought that would be the end of it. But as soon as he sat down on their first day back after break, he knew something weird was going on and he wasn't the only one who noticed it.

Vern, who sat behind him, tapped his shoulder then leaned forward and whispered, "Chewbacca is staring at you."

Fitch already knew that. She was looking at him like she was waiting for something. For what? He didn't know. Eye contact, maybe, so she could talk to him.

He kept his eyes forward.

"Hey . . . " she said. Quiet. "Henry?"

Ugh. No one at school called him Henry except substitute teachers. *No one.*

Eyes forward. Avoid eye contact.

Ms. Salonga closed the door as Rachel Hill— always the last to arrive, always smiling and smelling like bubble gum, always a side ponytail draped across her delicate shoulder—breezed in and took her seat.

Why couldn't *Rachel Hill* give him a laser stare? Why did it have to be Amanda?

A louder whisper: "Hey. Henry?"

He had no choice. He had to look at her. When he did, she smiled and reached over the aisle with something in her hand.

Oh god. Was it a note?

No, it was a sticker the size of his palm. Darth Vader clutching his lightsaber with both hands. The saber glowed bright red against Vader's black robes. It was a pretty cool sticker, but not worth the price he was gonna pay. He could practically feel Vern's laughter behind him.

"For your notebook," Amanda said.

The sticker may as well have been a ball of fire. He dropped it on his desk and roiled with conflicting emotions. Embarrassment, dread, mortification, and yes, guilt. Guilt because it was a nice gesture—the first gesture a girl had ever showed him, actually—and he wanted no part of it.

"Thanks," he mumbled.

He slid the sticker between the pages of his notebook and focused on Ms. Salonga, who was writing a date on the board: January 23, 1986. Underneath she wrote *"Challenger* Launch!" in her distinctly loopy handwriting.

She tapped the board with her chalk.

"I hope you're ready for liftoff," she said.

NOT A PRETTY THOUGHT

Sometimes Bird wished Ms. Salonga was her mother. It wasn't a pretty thought, but there it was.

There was nothing *wrong* with Tammy Nelson

Thomas, who insisted that all her children have her maiden name as their middle names, who complained about work all the time, who constantly "watched her weight," but she was a squeaky gear and Ms. Salonga was so . . . even-tempered. Calm. Predictable. Ms. Salonga was organized and often talked about "best-laid plans" and their importance to science. She had even applied for the Teacher in Space program. Ms. Salonga had told the story many times.

It went like this: Ms. Salonga and her family ate dinner together every night. There was a rule that no one could argue at the dinner table, and everyone had to listen to what everyone else said. Despite these rules (which seemed beautifully foreign and mysterious to Bird), Ms. Salonga didn't expect a warm reaction when she said she wanted to be the first teacher in space. She imagined all the things her husband and children would say: *Space! You don't even like to ride the Ferris wheel!* Or *You, an astronaut?*

Get serious! But she underestimated them. They were excited. They asked a million questions and Ms. Salonga answered each one, all while they passed mashed potatoes and chicken around. The following week, they got her a card. On the front it said "Good Luck!" and inside they wrote: "To the first teacher in space and our favorite astronaut!"

At this point in the story, Ms. Salonga would pause and say, "People are full of surprises."

Generally, Bird did not like surprises. But she wouldn't mind a surprise like that.

Ms. Salonga kept the card on her desk, standing upright, even though they all knew that her application had not been accepted and that she wouldn't be the first teacher in space after all. President Reagan had picked Christa McAuliffe instead.

That didn't dampen Ms. Salonga's enthusiasm for space travel one bit.

Today, as promised, she was launching Space

Month! As part of Space Month!, the class would be split into three separate flight crews with jobs that mirrored those on the space shuttle *Challenger*.

"There are seven possible job assignments per crew," Ms. Salonga said. "Each crew has one pilot, one shuttle commander, three mission specialists, and two payload specialists." She lifted a small paper bag and shook it. "All the jobs are in this bag. Reach in *without looking*. Pick *one*."

Bird's leg shook under her desk when Ms. Salonga arrived at her row. She closed her eyes and repeated the same two words over and over: *shuttle commander, shuttle commander, shuttle commander.* If she said it three times, maybe she could wish it into being.

Devonte Harris, who sat in front of her, reached in the bag and rifled around with his tongue sticking out. Bird tried to read the sliver of paper over his shoulder, but Ms. Salonga quickly moved on and blocked her view.

"Your turn, Bird," she said, smiling.

Bird crossed the fingers on her right hand and reached into the bag with her left. Her fingertips brushed the scraps. They all felt the same. Finally she pulled one out.

mission specialist

Bird frowned. She hoped Ms. Salonga would feel bad enough to let her choose again, but instead she moved on to Danielle Logan.

Bird didn't want to be a mission specialist. She wanted to be shuttle commander. The shuttle commander was the person in charge, the person who made sure all the machines worked properly.

Devonte turned around.

"What'd you get?" he asked.

"Mission specialist."

"I got pilot, if you wanna trade. I know it's not shuttle commander, but . . . "

Bird was about to agree and hand over her paper, but it didn't seem fair. Pilot would have been her second choice, but if she traded, then it really wouldn't be random the way Ms. Salonga intended, and rules made for best-laid plans. Usually.

"It's okay," Bird said. "Thanks anyway."

The room buzzed once everyone had their job assignments. Ms. Salonga asked all the shuttle commanders to stand. Bird tried not to be jealous, especially when Danielle Logan stood, but she couldn't help it.

The other astronauts were assigned to the commander nearest them so Bird and Devonte wound up on Danielle's shuttle with mission specialist Christopher-not-Chris Wheeler, mission specialist Marcus Sturgess, and payload specialists Jessica Brantley and Jessica Diaz, best friends of Rachel Hill—a.k.a., the most popular girl in school. Jessica Brantley was called "JB" when on her own. When with her best friend, which was virtually all the time, they were known collectively as The Jessicas. JB's older brother Brant was on the basketball team and one of Cash's best friends. (Bird thought Brant was a jerk, but she kept that information to herself.)

Throughout January, Ms. Salonga explained, the crews would be given problem-solving missions. They'd have to work through the missions together.

"Your first two tasks are to decide why you are going into space, and what you'll name your space shuttle," she said.

Desks were shoved together, scraping against the classroom floor, as the crews moved into huddles.

Danielle, who everyone called "Dani," greeted her crew with a smile that showed nearly all her teeth.

"Any thoughts on a name for our spaceship?" she asked.

Bird liked Dani Logan. Dani was nice and

always had extra pencils for people to borrow. But at that moment, Bird had some not-pretty thoughts about her role as shuttle commander.

"Space *shuttle*," Bird corrected.

"Space shuttle," Dani repeated.

"What about . . . *The Madonna*?" Jessica Diaz said, eyes shining. Other Jessica nodded enthusiastically.

"No way," Devontc said.

Jessica Brantley shot up straight and swung her blond hair off her shoulders. "I got it, I got it! *Lucky Star!*"

"Isn't that a Madonna song?" Christopher-not-Chris said. His hair hung in his eyes. Some of the strands caught in his eyelashes and fluttered when he blinked. Christopher-not-Chris wore rock band T-shirts just about every day. Today it was Van Halen.

"Yeah," Jessica said. "So?"

"I'm not gonna be part of a ship that's named after Madonna," he said.

Marcus, who barely spoke in class and seemed to be absent at least once every week, lifted an unenthusiastic finger. "I second that," he said.

The Jessicas huffed and rolled their eyes.

"Dani should get the final say," said Jessica Brantley. "She's the shuttle commander."

They all turned to Dani.

Dani turned to Bird.

"Do you have any suggestions, Bird?" she said.

Of course she did.

"How about *Bright Star One*?" When no one said anything, she added, "It's a pinball machine at the arcade on Main."

"*Bright Star One*," Dani repeated, trying it on for size.

"I like it," Devonte said.

"Me, too," said the Jessicas.

Christopher-not-Chris and Marcus both shrugged. They didn't seem to care, as long as the shuttle wasn't named after Madonna.

The mission of *Bright Star One* was easily

decided: They were going to study Halley's Comet, just like the *Challenger* astronauts.

When the bell rang, Dani raised both her arms in a victory pose and shouted, *"Bright Star One to space!"* at the top of her lungs and everyone laughed—not *at* her, but *with* her—because, like Bird, they knew it was all in good fun, and no one was really going into outer space like the *Challenger* crew, no matter how badly they wanted to.

THIS IS THE PINBALL WIZARD

There was a time when the Nelson Thomas family orbited the same sun, but that was in the distant past. They'd drifted apart at some point, but no one knew when or how. One thing was certain, however: the Nelson Thomas siblings always, without fail, went their separate ways as soon as the bell rang.

Cash usually went with his friends.

Bird went home.

And Fitch walked to the arcade with Vern. They had an instinctual habit of looking for discarded coins while they navigated the sidewalk, but today Vern shoved Fitch hard in the shoulder as they made their way down the street and said, "Chewbacca is in love with you!"

The sticker incident had happened during first period, which seemed like an eternity ago, so Fitch thought it'd escaped his best friend's attention.

No such luck.

"Chewbacca *loves* you!" said Vern. He puckered his lips and made kissy noises.

The fire in Fitch's chest sparked. "Shut up," he said.

At least he hadn't ended up on the same

stupid "shuttle crew" as Amanda. *That* would have been a nightmare.

They approached the gas station and raced to the pay phone to check for quarters, but the slot was bare.

Fitch had only fifty cents on him, which he'd pocketed instead of getting lunch, and he sensed that it wouldn't be his lucky day once they got to the Pinball Wizard.

He was right.

The place was crowded. Major Havoc was taken. Same for all the *Star Wars* games, Pole Position, Karate Champ, and Centipede. Kids were everywhere, little kids, shrieking and yelling and running, and there were so many games going at once that the sounds melded together into one chaotic melody. Some dork with glasses was playing Pop-A-Shot and missed every basket. A group of bigger boys howled each time the dork aimed for a new one, which only made things worse. All those wasted quarters, Fitch thought.

Mr. Hindley wove in and out of the crowd, beaming from ear to ear. When he saw Fitch, he walked up to him and said, "Gotta love seeing all this business."

"Not me," said Fitch. He nodded toward Major Havoc. "My game's taken."

Mr. Hindley nudged him. "You could always kill time on one of my pinball machines. This is the Pinball Wizard, after all."

"Your pinball machine stole my quarter yesterday."

Mr. Hindley nodded regretfully. "I need to get that one fixed. Hate seeing 'Out of Order' signs in my shop." He dug into his pocket and handed Fitch a quarter. "We're even now. Knock yourself out. If you can find an open game."

He smacked Fitch on the back. As he walked away, Vern said, "As long as you're giving out quarters, Mr. Hindley, I'll take one! Donkey Kong ate my fifty cents two weeks ago!"

Fitch ran his fingers around the edge of his

new quarter as if it were a lump of gold.

Mr. Hindley kept walking.

"I'm serious, Mr. Hindley!" Vern continued. "That ape is a thief!"

Mr. Hindley waved him off without turning around.

Vern shrugged. "It was worth a shot."

One of the reasons Fitch loved Major Havoc was that it felt like *his*. Most of the other kids thought the game was too complicated, too hard to figure out, and they didn't care about the backstory at all. Instead, they beelined toward the more popular games and left Major Havoc to fend for himself. Usually the Major was ready and waiting for Fitch. No one else at the controls. But now, as he and Vern stood just a few feet away, surveying the room, Fitch watched some tall kid with Keds play *his* game, die, then put in another quarter.

"Let's go lean," said Vern, which meant he wanted to walk over to the wall near the pinball machines, hang out, and act casual.

Fitch shoved the quarter deep into his pocket.

Ever since Fitch got to middle school last year, he had the sense that everything was about acting casual no matter what, like nothing in the world mattered and you couldn't be bothered to care about anything, even though everyone cared about everything.

He and Vern went to the wall and leaned.

"So, seriously, dude. What are you gonna do about Chewbacca?" Vern said.

"Stop calling her that."

"Why?" Sly grin. "You love her or something?"

"No." And he didn't—not at all. It bothered him, though, the way Vern said "Chewbacca." It felt like a joke against him instead of Amanda. Or maybe it was a joke on both of them. Who could tell? The point was, he was part of a joke.

"Then what do you care?" said Vern. He paused. "So, whatcha gonna do?"

"What do you mean, what am I gonna do? Nothing."

Vern looked as though he was about to say something else when Justin Brantley and Kenny Haskins walked up.

"Hey, what's going on with your brother?" said Brant, nodding at Fitch. "I haven't seen him since his Olympic slip on the ice."

"He stayed home today because of his cast."

"That idiot," Brant said, laughing. "You should've seen him go down. Man! It looked like it hurt." He glanced from Fitch to Vern and back again. "What're you two talking about, anyway?"

Fitch and Vern spoke at the same time.

Fitch said, "Nothing."

Vern said, "Chewbacca is in love with Fitch."

"Chewbacca?" said Kenny, raising an eyebrow.

"Yeah," Vern replied. "Amanda Piper."

Fitch's eyes wandered to Major Havoc. When would that tall kid leave so he could play? He imagined walking over and pushing him aside. He imagined the kid stumbling over his Keds as Fitch took the controls.

"Amanda Piper, Amanda Piper . . ." said Brant. "Oh, wait. Is she a seventh-grader with, like, bushy brown hair and a big enormous head?"

Vern laughed and laughed like this was the funniest thing anyone had ever said. He often did that around Brant and Kenny because they were part of a more popular crowd. Brant and Kenny were kings at acting casual.

"Yeah, that's her," Vern said. "She's in love with Fitch. She's so in love with him that she calls him by his real name. Right, *Henry*?" He nudged Fitch in the ribs.

That's when the fire popped and burst and, in one swift movement that no one saw coming, Fitch wrapped his hand around Vern's wrist— tight, tight—and pushed him back a step.

"Don't touch me again," Fitch said.

His eyes were so fiery and his voice so angry that Vern simply nodded and winced. When Fitch let him go, Vern rubbed his wrist like someone who had just been released from handcuffs.

"Jesus, man," Vern said. "Calm down."

Yes, Fitch. Calm down. Calm down.

Fitch wanted to apologize, especially since Cash's friends were looking at him like he was a mental patient, but the words wouldn't come out of his mouth. Instead he stood there until Major Havoc was finally free, and then he walked away without another word.

FROZEN
BY MUMM-RA

It would've been nice if someone had stayed home with him, since it was his first day with a cast and his wrist still hurt and he had trouble doing normal stuff, like going to the bathroom or opening a bag of chips, but it was what it was.

Cash spent most of the time sleeping, staring at the television (he wasn't really watching, since it was mostly game shows and soap operas), reading the sports section of the *Philadelphia Inquirer*, and eating junk food. His mother called in the early afternoon to make sure he was still alive and to say that she would be late because someone called an afternoon meeting, and wouldn't you just know someone would call an afternoon meeting on the *very day* she needed to be home early.

Bird got home first. When she walked in, he was sprawled on the couch, watching *He-Man and the Masters of the Universe*. He was too old for it, but so what?

"How's your arm?" she asked. She set her backpack on one of the stools at the kitchen island and opened the fridge. "You want something to drink?"

"Nah," said Cash. He was being very still, for no particular reason except that he wanted to be as lazy as humanly possible. He didn't move until Bird came to sit down. And he didn't move much—just slid his feet over.

She took a big gulp of Diet Coke, then wiped the corners of her mouth with her knuckle. "I don't have your assignments because Mom said Fitch had to pick them up for you instead, since you have more of the same teachers."

"Okay," said Cash. He'd forgotten that Bird had offered to do that for him.

"Ms. Salonga's class was awesome. She separated everyone into flight crews, just like the *Challenger*."

Cash's eyes were glued to the television, so he was only half listening. The father in this toy commercial had a mustache. Cash wondered if he would ever grow hair on his face. He wanted to brush above his lip to see if anything had grown while he'd been on the couch, but he was still trying not to move.

"Just like the what?" he said.

"The *Challenger*. You know. The space shuttle?"

"Oh, yeah. Space month."

"Yep. I wanted to be shuttle commander, but Dani Logan got it instead, so I'm a mission specialist. We named our shuttle *Bright Star One*, after the pinball game. And our mission is to study Halley's Comet, just like the astronauts."

It was quiet for a while, so Cash finally said, "Cool."

"I suggested *Bright Star One* as the name. Everyone liked it."

"Mm-hm."

"At first I was jealous of Dani, but I think she'll be a good shuttle commander."

"Yeah."

Bird sipped her soda. "Do you need anything for your arm?"

"Nah."

Bird stared at the television.

ThunderCats was coming on, which meant it was four-thirty. *You're too old to watch ThunderCats,* Cash reminded himself.

"Where's Fitch?" Cash asked.

It was a stupid question.

"Arcade."

Tammy and Mike Thomas expected all three children to be home when they walked through the door. They usually were. Tammy and Mike Thomas also expected all homework to be done. It usually wasn't. But they never actually checked any of these things. They'd ask if everyone had finished their homework and Cash and Fitch would say yes, even though they hadn't, and Bird would say yes or no, but it didn't matter because they all knew Bird would get her work done no matter what.

Fitch came home at the same time *ThunderCats* ended. He gave an obligatory "hey" before disappearing into his room.

Thirty minutes later their father came in. He didn't give an obligatory "hey." Instead he asked, "Where's your mother?"

Bird had gone to her room, so Cash was alone again on the couch, still in the same position.

The news was on, and he hated the news, but he decided he'd been permanently frozen by Mumm-Ra, demon priest of the *ThunderCats* universe.

"She called to say she'd be late," Cash said.

His father sighed. "How late?"

"I don't know. A meeting or something."

"Figures," his father mumbled.

Cash couldn't see his father, but he knew he was standing in the middle of the kitchen with his hands on his hips. That was the weird thing about families. Sometimes you just knew what your family was up to, even if you couldn't see them.

THE RULES OF LANGUAGE

The problem was dinner.

When their mother got home, it was 6:40 and

no one had eaten. Their mother was usually the one who made dinner, so their father said they would wait for her.

That was a mistake.

Bird knew it was a mistake. She could predict an argument a mile away. Nothing could be done about it, though. Bird didn't know how to cook, so it's not like she could prepare a meal for them. Instead she did the next best thing: she ate a turkey sandwich. That way her mom wouldn't have to worry about including her. She suggested that the others eat sandwiches, too, but they said no, they wanted to wait for something good.

So Bird went into her room and waited, too.

But not for something good.

Rules of language were different for kids than adults. Bird learned this early on.

For example: neither Bird nor her brothers were allowed to curse. Certainly not in front of their parents. Not even the safe swears that weren't super-bad, like h-e-double-hockey-sticks. If they said something "uncouth," as her mother would say, their father would blurt out, "Language!" as a reminder that they were using bad words.

No such rules applied to Mr. and Mrs. Thomas. They were allowed to use *all* the words. They could even pair some of the words together, like when Mr. Thomas called Mrs. Thomas a "stupid [expletive] cow," or when she called him a "moronic [expletive] [expletive]." Every ugly word was on the table—especially when they spoke to each other.

Bird listened to them now, with her ear pressed against the door. She didn't want to but couldn't help it. There was little reason to put her ear there, though. They were yelling so that she could have been standing in the driveway and heard everything. But at least she was doing something.

Tammy was calling Mike "a stupid Neanderthal idiot."

Mike was calling Tammy "a nagging pain in the [expletive]."

Tammy said she shouldn't have to work all day and then come home and cook dinner when Mike had "two perfectly good arms and legs."

Mike said it was her fault. She was the one who refused to "clean up the [expletive] house" and wanted to get a job so she "could feel like Gloria [expletive] Steinman," to which Tammy replied, "It's Gloria *Steinem,* you [expletive], and the very fact that you *expect* me to make you dinner after I worked harder and longer than you is *disgusting!*"

"Of course I expected dinner!" said Mike. "You're clearly not doing much else in this house! And you've made dinner for the past fifteen years!"

"And that's exactly the problem!"

"If you didn't want to make dinner, all you had to do was say, 'Mike, I'm too tired to make dinner.'" (At this point, Mike did his pretend-Tammy voice, which wasn't flattering at all.) "You didn't have to explode in front of the [expletive] kids!"

"Oh, so now I'm a bad parent!"

At some point during their arguments, if they went on long enough, one of them would accuse the other of being a bad parent. That's when the fights—or "disagreements," as their parents called them—would get really ugly. They never hit each other. Instead they knocked things around the house. He might throw her book across the room and she might kick the kitchen chair until it broke, for example.

Bird wasn't in the mood for broken chairs and tossed books.

Cash and Fitch had disappeared into their rooms back when the argument was a slow simmer, and she couldn't blame them. She would have done the same thing, if she hadn't already been in hers. Once their kids were out of sight, Mr. and Mrs. Thomas morphed into their own separate machine. One that shot sparks and burned skin.

Someone needed to stick a screwdriver in the spokes.

Bird took a deep breath and turned the knob.

But someone else beat her to it.

Fitch. His door flew open with such force that it shook hers.

"*WHY DID YOU EVEN [EXPLETIVE] GET MARRIED?*" he yelled.

Bird's heart stopped beating.

The refrigerator door swung open and slammed shut. All the jars rattled. Fitch went back to his room. *SLAM!* One second later he turned on his radio. The volume went up, up, up. "Walking on the Moon" by the Police.

Bird sat down, right where she was standing, still facing her door.

She wondered what her parents were doing. She couldn't hear them anymore.

All she heard was the music.

My feet don't hardly make no sound
Walking on, walking on the moon.

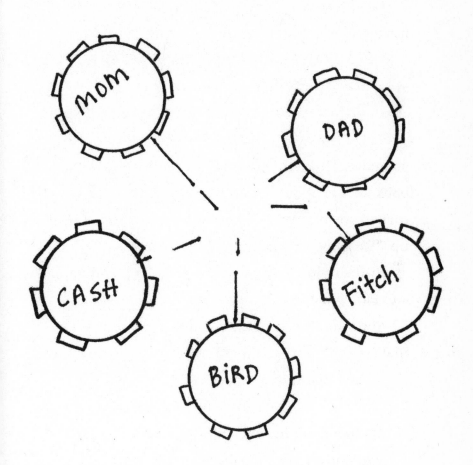

TOMORROW

Cash kept dreaming about his arm. He dreamed he was a rock climber. He dreamed he played the drums. He dreamed he shot hoops. In his dreams, he did all this with one hand.

On Sunday night, when the house was still and quiet, he woke up thinking he was on the court with the Sixers and the Rockets, but he was just in his bed with an aching arm. It itched and he had to use a wire hanger to reach inside the cast and scratch.

He didn't want to do anything but lie around.

He hadn't left the house all weekend. He'd even missed school again Friday, and Fitch had forgotten to pick up some of his assignments. It didn't matter, though. He was already way behind and now he'd probably flunk all over again. When he thought about being a grade behind his two younger siblings, it made a knot in his stomach that got tighter and tighter until he didn't want to move.

Tomorrow he'd have to go back to school. There was no way around it.

Dr. J was poised to take a shot from the poster on the door. The Sixers had lost to Houston on Saturday night by fifteen points. It was disappointing, but you win some, you lose some. That's what Cash's dad always said. He only said it when something was being lost.

Cash had Monday all planned out in his head.

What did Ms. Salonga call it?

Best-laid plans.

Yes, that was it.

He had his *best-laid plans.*

They all centered around Penny.

They went like this:

1. Get signatures on his cast.

2. Get *good* signatures only. Brant and Kenny were solid. And his locker was near Rachel Hill, so he'd ask her, too. And maybe some of her friends. He wanted a mix of boys and girls.

3. Once the signatures were in place, take his seat in Ms. Salonga's class, all casual, and wait for Penny.

4. Don't look too anxious. Act like it's any other Monday. If he was lucky, Penny would notice the cast right away and ask what happened. In which case:

5. Offer the marker to Penny and ask her to sign his cast. As she's signing (and noticing the popular names on his cast), that's when he would—

6. Talk to her. Like, a real conversation.

It was a good plan.

"Tomorrow, Dr. J," Cash said, to the poster. "You have my word."

HEY, HENRY

When Fitch was four years old, he threw a tantrum in Toys R Us. Bird blinked up at their mother and said, "He is really fitching a pit!" And it made everyone laugh, including him. They called him "Fitch" from that point on, just like they called Bernadette "Bird" because he couldn't pronounce her name when they were little. He and Bird were twins, and they had named each other, for better or worse.

But Amanda kept calling him "Henry."

When he walked into Ms. Salonga's class on Monday morning: "Hey, Henry."

When Ms. Salonga told them to open their science books to page one-twenty: "What page did she say, Henry?"

When the bell rang: "What'd you do this weekend, Henry?"

"No one calls me that," Fitch finally said, jaw twitching, as they gathered their books. He'd answered all her questions as politely as he could, but if she called him Henry one more time, he wasn't sure what would happen.

"I know," said Amanda. She smiled. "I just like calling you Henry."

Vern stifled laughter as he navigated his Trapper Keeper into his backpack. Then he opened his mouth.

"Do *you* have any nicknames, Amanda?" Vern asked.

Amanda raised her eyebrows. "Me? Oh. Sometimes my dad calls me Mandy."

Vern swatted Fitch's arm. "Mandy and Henry," he said. "It almost rhymes."

A PERFECT
SPOT
FOR PENNY

By the time Ms. Salonga's third-period class rolled around, Cash had signatures from most of the social elite of Park Middle School. He'd had to answer the same question again and again—*What happened? What happened?*—and sometimes it hurt when he moved his arm a certain way so someone could sign a particular spot, but it was worth it. He had plenty of signatures, and there was still a perfectly placed spot for Penny. He could not have planned it better.

She walked in on cue. He made eye contact, but not too much. He smiled, but not too much. He scratched the tip of his nose the moment he knew her eyes were on him so she'd get full view of his injury.

She gasped as she slung her backpack off her shoulder. "What happened?"

Cash shrugged. *Act casual.* "I fell and broke my wrist."

"Did it hurt?"

"Nah." That was a lie—it *still* hurt, now and then—but he couldn't really admit that, could he?

Penny situated her books. He waited for his plan to unfold, but the seconds inched by and nothing happened. Class would start soon. He needed to do something before she turned her full attention to Ms. Salonga.

"Do you wanna sign it?" he blurted out. He held up his marker, dropped it, picked it up. "My cast, I mean."

"Oh. Sure!" Penny smiled. The freckles on her nose crinkled.

Cash's belly flipped.

Their fingers touched when she took the marker from him.

His skin tingled.

He leaned forward to bring the cast closer to her and she reached over the back of her chair to write. The smell of fresh marker drifted in the air.

"The worst part is, I can't take notes," he said.

Penny didn't look up. "Did you have Ms. Salonga last year? Maybe you can use your old notes."

Cash cleared his throat. His neck warmed.

"Oh," he said. "No, I had Mr. Duncan."

"Just a thought." She snapped the cap back on and said, "Voilá!"

Cash looked down. He saw her signature right away, exactly where he'd wanted it. Loopy. A single "i" dotted with a heart. It was upside down from his vantage point, but yes, there it was:

Penny L/S Charlie

Cash wasn't fluent in romantic middle school shorthand, but he knew what L/S meant. *Penny Loves Charlie.*

Penny Loves Charlie, right there on his arm.

"Charlie who?" Cash asked, hoping his voice wasn't laced with disappointment or—even worse—jealousy.

"Charlie Gowan," she said, matter-of-fact. "He's in eighth grade. Do you know him?"

Charlie Gowan. Charlie Gowan. Charlie Gowan. A face came into view. Brown hair. Honors student. They'd never had any classes together, of course. Charlie Gowan was a smart kid and he . . . well, he was Cash Nelson Thomas, the boy who failed seventh grade.

"Yeah," Cash said. "I think so."

The tardy bell rang. Penny turned around. The smell of her shampoo wafted up Cash's nose.

He sat back.

Maybe you can use your old notes.

She knew he'd flunked. Of course she knew. What other kid at Park Middle School was in the same grade as his younger brother and sister?

And now she loved Charlie Gowan.

Would *Charlie* have saved space on his cast for her?

Cash averted his eyes from Penny's hair. He wouldn't look. If she wanted to go around with some honors student, so be it. What did he care? He had laughed it up with Rachel Hill just that morning in the hall, and she was the most popular girl in school. He didn't need *Penny* and her stupid *honors boyfriend.*

If she liked smart guys, that was her business.

School was stupid anyway. Ms. Salonga had them on imaginary crews going to space. For what purpose? None of them were ever *going* to space. What was the point?

He cradled his arm closer as Ms. Salonga wrote "Halley's Comet" on the chalkboard.

Seriously.

What was the point of any of it?

OPTICAL ILLUSION

Stars were always moving, Ms. Salonga said. Constellations were an optical illusion, in a way. They seemed to stay the same, but really, each star was moving at high speed. Some were careening toward each other. Some were shooting in opposite directions.

"The only reason we can't tell is because we're so far away," Ms. Salonga said. "But in fifty thousand years, the Big Dipper will look very different."

There were other illusions, too, according to Ms. Salonga. Some of the light in the night sky didn't even exist.

"Light takes time to travel long distances," she said. "By the time it gets to us, it may not even be there anymore. And speaking of long distances . . ."

She erased the vocabulary words she'd written on the board at the beginning of the period and replaced them with "Halley's Comet." She tossed the chalk from hand to hand, which she often did when she was excited about a particular topic. Space was worthy of a lot of chalk tossing, Bird noticed. It was contagious, too. Bird found herself tapping the eraser of her pencil on her notebook.

Ms. Salonga scanned the classroom.

"As you know, one of the missions of the *Challenger* expedition is to observe Halley's Comet." She paused. "Devonte, can you tell us what comets are made of?"

When Devonte didn't answer right away, Bird whispered "ice" as quietly as she could, and without moving her mouth. Like a ventriloquist.

"Ice!" Devonte said. "And"—he raised a ceremonious index finger—"dust particles."

Ms. Salonga nodded proudly. "Very good, Mr. Harris."

When Ms. Salonga walked toward her desk to pick up a stack of handouts, Devonte threw a thumbs-up in Bird's direction.

"I want all of you to learn the names of your counterparts on the *Challenger*," Ms. Salonga was saying, her photocopies now in the crook of her arm. "Names *and* titles of everyone on board. And I want to know what you'll be doing, individually, to contribute to your missions. Use the remainder of the class to discuss this with your flight crew."

The students immediately got out of their desks and, in a chorus of scrapes and chatter, moved into semicircles with their fellow astronauts as Ms. Salonga gave each of them a handout.

Bird studied her photocopy as soon as she was seated with the rest of *Bright Star One*. "The *Challenger* Crew," it said across the top. There was a black-and-white photo of each astronaut. They were smiling, wearing identical flight suits, and holding helmets. There were only two female astronauts—the teacher, Christa McAuliffe, who was listed as a "payload specialist," and Judith Resnik, a mission specialist.

Bird studied Judith Resnik, mission specialist. She had curly brown hair, brown eyes, freckles, and dimples. Bird also had those things. She'd never considered their similarities before. The line between Judith Resnik's face and Bird's face blurred until Bird saw herself sitting there in a jumpsuit, holding an astronaut's helmet.

She was lost in this image when Devonte snapped her out of it. Literally.

Snap, snap. "Earth to Bird," he said.

The crew of *Bright Star One* stared at her from their circle.

"You zoned out," Devonte said.

"Sorry." Bird shifted in her seat. "I was just thinking about Judith Resnik."

"Who's Judith Resnik?" Christopher asked.

"One of the mission specialists," Bird said.

"What about her?" Devonte asked.

"I was thinking about how much we look alike," said Bird. She held up the photocopy. The astronauts smiled from the paper. "Don't you think?"

The crew studied the photo.

"I guess," said Jessica Diaz. "But she's pretty."

The words came out casually. *But she's pretty.* Bird heard it again. *But she's pretty.* That word—"but." What did that mean?

"I mean, it's not that you're *not* pretty, Bird," said Jessica, quickly. "Just . . . well." She looked at everyone else in the circle. "Being pretty really isn't your thing." She shrugged, as if this concluded the whole conversation.

Not her thing?

"Being smart is your thing," Jessica explained.

An awkward cloud of tension floated over them and hovered there until Ms. Salonga started speaking again.

"This is how the astronauts will be seated when they board the shuttle for takeoff," Ms. Salonga said, drawing circles on the board. "Astronauts Scobee and Smith are in seats one and two, on the flight deck, with Onizuka and Resnik behind them. The remaining seats are on middeck. That's where McAuliffe, McNair, and Jarvis will be. Everyone in this room should know those names." She raised her eyebrows, as if to say: *right?* Collective and tentative nods moved through the room. "The seating arrangement will be slightly modified when they come back for landing. But for now, I want you to arrange your desks according to this seating chart, with all of you facing the board."

Bird stood quickly. Jessica's words were still there, drifting and buzzing, even if no one could hear them anymore but her.

"I'm a payload specialist," JB whispered. Bird couldn't tell if she was talking to her or someone else. "Which seat is for the payload specialist?"

Bird knew the answer, of course. The payload specialists sat on middeck. But she didn't want to answer. She wasn't sure if she wanted "smart" to be her *thing* just now.

Once everyone took their seats, Ms. Salonga weaved through the desks to make sure they'd arranged themselves correctly. The class was silent in their unfamiliar, staggered rows.

"Now," Ms. Salonga said, walking from the back of the room to the front. "I want all of you to close your eyes."

Bird did.

Moments passed.

"I'm serious, Marcus—close your eyes," said Ms. Salonga.

Kids snickered. Not Bird.

"Okay," Ms. Salonga continued. "Now I want you to imagine that you're not in your desk at all. You're not in Delaware. You're in Houston, Texas. You're strapped tight to your chair, on your back, pointed to the sky. You've got your helmet on. What do you hear?"

Someone made an obscene sound. More snickers.

Bird had her eyes closed tight, so she couldn't

see if Ms. Salonga reacted. If so, she didn't say anything aloud. Instead she went on: "Think about it. What do you hear?"

Bird heard the crackle through her nonexistent headset. Mission control, mixed with Ms. Salonga's voice. Perhaps Ms. Salonga was working in Houston, like all those men in their button-up shirts and ties, except she's wearing her teacher clothes—her long skirt and blouse, with her dark hair in a banana clip—and she is leaning over a switchboard, saying "Houston to *Challenger*. Do you copy, Mission Specialist Thomas?"

Yes, said Bird. *I copy.*

"The first thing you have to do is complete your series of preflight checks," Ms. Salonga said. "Once all your preflight checks are complete, you'll have to—eyes *closed,* Jessica Diaz—wait for the crew to finish final rocket preparations. Your heart is pounding in your ears. There's something you keep wondering about—stop that, Christopher, I see what you're doing—and what you wonder is: What will it look like up there? What will it *feel* like?"

Preflight check is complete.

Final rocket preparations complete.

Bird clutched her hands on the side of her seat.

She knew what it would look like. From up there, Earth would look like a bright blue ball, glowing in the darkness just for her.

She knew what it would feel like, too. In the summers she and her brothers sometimes went to the community pool. She would go underwater and stay there for as long as she could. It was like she was suspended midway in the universe—not exactly standing on two feet, not exactly floating in midair. That's what space would feel like.

The headset crackled.

"All systems are go," Ms. Salonga said. "The engines are powered."

The floor rumbled underneath Bird, as if a giant beast was waking up. Engine systems, pressurized. The shuttle thumped and bumped with the opening and closing of valves. The rumble grew from the floor to the chair to the backs of Bird's thighs. The world shook, shook, shook—so hard Bird felt it in every bone in her body.

"As the shuttle gears up for launch, the force of gravity against your body increases," Ms. Salonga said. "This is called the 'g-load.' There's a big push forward, and the g-load builds. Suddenly you're in the air."

Yes, she was in the air. Unmoored. At this moment, nothing bound her to this Earth.

"You hear the rockets jettison from the spacecraft."

Yes, Bird could hear them. Go, go. All she needed was the shuttle.

"And just like that—you're in space. All that force you felt before, when you thought your face might melt right into the seat? It's gone. There's nothing holding you down but your harness. Everything is floating, including you."

The Earth becomes so small, like the head of

a pin or a grain of sand. The Earth is round and blue and beautiful and everything is far away. Out here, no one is pretty. Everyone is pretty. No one is smart. Everyone is smart.

Out here, there is only you.

Copy. Copy.

Dani Logan's voice drifted in from the periphery.

"Hey, Bird?" she said. "I was wondering if you wanted to come over after school tomorrow. You can walk home with me. You know, if you want."

Bird opened her eyes. She was the only one still sitting in her chair. Everyone—including Dani—had already put their desks back where they belonged. People were leaving for the next class. When had the bell rung? Bird hadn't even heard it.

Jessica's words still floated in the air, but Bird was floating, too. She was Mission Specialist Thomas, and she'd just arrived home from the space shuttle *Challenger*. Who could think about anything else at a time like this?

Everyone, apparently.

The classroom was just as it always was, and so were its inhabitants. They moved around her as if she hadn't just spent the past few minutes with her eyes sealed shut, lost in another world.

Bird got up. Pushed her desk back where it belonged. The sound of the chair legs scraping against linoleum brought her back to the cold, hard floor of Park Middle School.

"If not, it's no big deal," said Dani.

"What's no big deal?" Bird said.

"I asked if you wanted to come over after school sometime."

"Oh," said Bird.

Was she still in another galaxy? This was the first time since she'd started middle school that someone had invited her over. She'd always been a girl who had in-school friends and sat with different tables at lunch depending on her mood. No best friend. No sleepovers. Just Bird.

But if she could shoot off into space on the *Challenger* next to Judith Resnik without ever leaving Park, Delaware, surely she could launch herself to Danielle Logan's house.

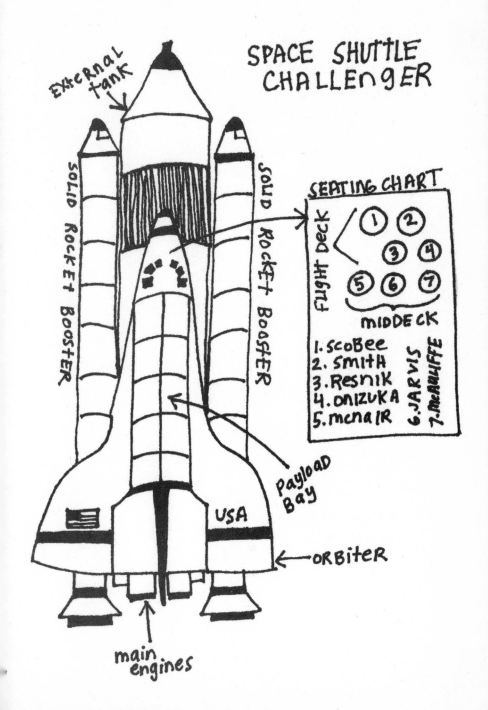

SPACE SHUTTLE CHALLENGER

External tank

SOLID ROCKET BOOSTER

SOLID ROCKET BOOSTER

SEATING CHART

FLIGHT DECK

① ②
③ ④
⑤ ⑥ ⑦

MIDDECK

1. SCOBEE
2. SMITH
3. RESNIK
4. ONIZUKA
5. MCNAIR
6. JARVIS
7. MCAULIFFE

Payload Bay

USA

← ORBITER

main engines

THE LOGAN FAMILY MACHINE

If Bird had to describe the way her house smelled, she would say it was the scent of old paperbacks that had been on the shelf too long. And sometimes it smelled like ground beef sizzling on the stove because Mrs. Nelson Thomas cooked a lot of dishes that required ground beef.

Dani Logan's house smelled like neither of those things.

Everything about Dani Logan's house was different, right down to where they hid the spare key. It was really clever, as far as Bird was concerned. At the Nelson Thomases', the key was tucked into the mailbox—not exactly the most ingenious place to hide something. At the Logans', the key was hidden inside the removable door knocker.

Bird inhaled discreetly as she slipped off her shoes and placed them obediently by the door—one of the "house rules," Dani said, rolling her eyes—then followed her new friend into the house.

There were no piles to navigate. No land mines of sneakers and sandals. No laundry baskets lining the hallways. There was so much space, Bird could practically *feel* the air move.

"Let's go to the kitchen and pig out," said Dani.

Pig out.

The junk food adds up eventually, Bernadette. That's what her mother said anytime Bird reached for junk food. If Bird ever asked why her brothers could eat whatever they wanted, her mother had a ready answer: *They need it. They're growing boys.*

Dani pulled Cheetos and Doritos from the pantry and motioned for Bird to follow her to the living room, where she sat on the carpet and clustered the bags on top of the coffee table.

Bird sat next to her.

"I'm not supposed to eat in the living room," said Dani. "But . . ." She shrugged and shoved Doritos in her mouth.

Bird looked around. So much open space. So much room to move. A person could be comfortable here. There was a sliding glass door behind the dining room table that led into a fenced yard. The Thomases had a fenced yard, too, but no one went out there except Mr. Thomas, and only when he had to cut the grass, which he didn't do as often as he should, according to Bird's mother.

Just in front of the Logans' fence was an enormous tree with a ladder nailed to its trunk.

Some of the steps were broken or tilted. Bird couldn't see the treehouse from this vantage point, but the ladder had to lead somewhere.

"Do you have a treehouse back there?" she asked.

Dani glanced outside. "Yeah. Well, I used to. My dad built it a long time ago, but most of it has fallen apart. It's basically just pieces of wood nailed to a tree at this point."

"I always wanted a treehouse," said Bird.

"Me, too," Dani said. "That's why my dad built it."

Bird wondered what that was like, to want something and then get it. Especially something like a treehouse. Until now Bird thought treehouses only existed in books or television. An optical illusion, like Ms. Salonga's constellations.

And on the walls: photos of Dani and her parents. In one of them—a huge, framed photo over the television—they wore matching colors and smiled broadly for the camera. Bird couldn't remember the last time she stood next to her parents and brothers for a photo. For anything, actually.

Dani followed her gaze.

"I don't have any brothers or sisters. Just me," Dani said. "It must be awesome to have a twin, huh?" When Bird didn't respond, Dani said, "I have a cat, though."

Bird's attention shifted immediately. "Really?"

"Yep. His name is Chekov. He can be kinda shy sometimes, but he's around here somewhere." Dani craned her neck this way and that and made kissy noises. "Chekov! Chekov!" She popped a chip in her mouth and chewed. *Crunch, crunch.* "His name is actually Chekov Scotty McCoy, because we couldn't decide what to call him. I wanted to name him Chekov, my dad liked McCoy, and my mom wanted to call him Scotty. We argued about it all the way home from the shelter until my mom finally said we should reach a consensus and name him all three."

Consensus. When Bird's parents argued, one of them usually wound up leaving the house for a few hours. One time her mom stayed away overnight. Apparently they never came to a consensus, since their arguments often repeated themselves.

What a world Danielle Logan lived in. Treehouses and consensus.

"Those are interesting names for a cat," said Bird.

"They're from *Star Trek*." Dani stopped mid-crunch. "Don't tell me you've never seen *Wrath of Khan*."

"No. I think my brother did." Bird shrugged.

"You'd love it! It's in space, Bird. *Space!* They are actually *trekking* through the *stars* in *space!*"

"It's not real, though."

Now it was Dani who shrugged. "Who needs real? We're surrounded by real all the time."

Bird had no comeback for that.

Crunch, crunch.

"Was it a bad argument?" Bird asked.

"What? Oh. No. It wasn't really an *argument* argument. Mostly just joking around." Dani grabbed another Dorito. "I wound up winning anyway because Chekov is his first name, so that's what we call him mostly." She stood up. "Do you want a soda?"

"Sure," Bird said. She stared at the Logan family portrait as Dani disappeared back into the kitchen.

"Sunkist or Tab?" Dani called.

Bird never drank sodas at home unless they were diet. Too much sugar. Too many calories. *You won't stay skinny forever.*

"Sunkist," Bird said.

Something about the Logan family portrait reminded Bird of the *Challenger* photo. She wasn't sure what the connection was. The mind was a mysterious machine. Suddenly Bird was thinking about Judith Resnik.

Dani came back with the soda and called for Chekov again.

"He's such a funny cat," Dani said. "He only likes to come out if he knows the environment is safe."

Bird took a long, deep sip of her Sunkist. "I understand," she said.

TRACKBALL

Not all gamers were well equipped to use a trackball. The trackball was unwieldy, unpredictable, and almost impossible to control. A joystick was much easier. Joysticks only moved certain ways. Herky-jerky. But trackballs? Trackballs responded to the slightest movement, and if it rolled even a smidge too far, Major Havoc would never get where he needed to go. To succeed at Major Havoc, you had to master the trackball *and* the two buttons, one of which was used for firing and jumping, and the other for activating Major Havoc's shield, which you could only do once per life. Missile Command and Centipede were the only other trackball games at the Pinball Wizard, and no one had achieved any impressive scores on either.

Fitch was always ready to defend Major Havoc to kids like Vern, who thought Major Havoc was subpar to all the other machines—trackball or no trackball—but he stayed quiet about his personal success. It was like his own little secret. No need for bragging. No need for showboating, like Vern often did when he hit a high level on Star Wars or Donkey Kong or whatever. As soon as people knew you were good at something, they started expecting things from you, and Fitch was perfectly happy living in a world where nothing was expected of him.

Somehow, though, as he reached his highest score yet and escaped into Major Havoc's galaxy, he'd managed to invite an unexpected comrade into his otherwise solitary wormhole.

The comrade announced himself in the moment after Major Havoc died and before Fitch kicked the machine and spewed a curse word.

"You're awesome."

Fitch whipped around, his body burning with annoyance and adrenaline.

The kid in front of him was eight or nine, maybe. Fitch recognized him right away as the dork who'd been wasting his quarters at Pop-A-Shot last week. He was wearing a wrinkled T-shirt with E.T. on it, and Fitch suddenly remembered that *E.T.* was the last movie his family had seen together at the theater. Bird and his mom had cried at the end. Fitch would have cried, too, but neither Cash nor his father had shed a single tear, so Fitch willed his away.

"You're awesome," the kid repeated. He wore thick glasses with heavy frames. When they slid down his nose, he pushed them up with the knuckle of his thumb.

"Thanks," Fitch mumbled.

"That game's really hard," the kid said. "I never saw anyone get that far."

"Most people give up." Fitch reached into his pocket. He knew he was out of quarters, but he reached into his pocket anyway. A small, impossible part of him always hoped to feel the ridges of a wayward quarter in the recess of his jeans, but it never happened. The day he found a forgotten quarter would be the day he'd fly off in his own Catastrofighter.

"I just moved here from New Jersey. The arcade back home didn't have Major Havoc," the kid said. "I tried to play it when I first got here, but I died in two seconds flat. I'm not good on the trackball. I'm okay with Centipede, though. Kinda." He pushed up his glasses. "My name's Marshall. People call me Marsh."

Fitch craned his neck to look around the arcade.

"Do you think you could teach me sometime?" Marsh asked.

Oh geez.

"Huh?" Fitch said. He took a step away from the kid. The last thing he needed was some eight-year-old hanger-on.

"Maybe you could teach me how to play sometime." Marsh shrugged. "Just a thought."

A voice rose toward them in the distance.

"Fitch Nelson Thomas! Evil Vaxxian overlord!"

Vern. He knew how deeply Major Havoc hated the Vaxxian Empire, which is why he insisted on alluding to it in the most ridiculous ways.

Marsh's eyes shifted toward Vern, who was now striding their way, holding a bag of popcorn dotted with grease. Every now and then Mr. Hindley cranked up his ancient popcorn machine and gave away free bags, just because.

Vern nudged Fitch with his elbow as he licked butter from his fingers.

"Hey, *Henry*. Finally hanging out with people your own age, eh?" said Vern, lifting a chin at Marshall and laughing.

Marsh ignored him. Pushed up his glasses. "See you around."

"Yeah," said Fitch, dismissively. "See you around."

When Marshall was out of earshot, Vern said, "I bet that kid could see all the way to next year with those glasses. Maybe even the new millennium."

"Whatever, man," Fitch said. "I'm going home. Unless you got quarters you wanna give me?"

"No way," said Vern. He lowered his voice. "I'm about to put mine on Ms. Pac-Man."

"Ms. Pac-Man? I've never seen you play Pac-Man in your life, much less *Ms.*"

"Let's just say that a certain someone is playing Ms. Pac-Man *right now* and I've never wanted to be a pellet or a ghost so bad in my life."

Fitch took a few strides forward with Vern at his heels, then casually looked in the direction of Ms. Pac-Man, where Rachel Hill stood at the joystick, the Jessicas at either elbow, all side ponytails and ribbons. Then Fitch looked at the scoreboard. Not bad.

"This is my opportunity," said Vern, through a mouthful of popcorn.

"Opportunity for what?"

"To make my move. What do you think?"

"You?" Fitch laughed—one loud, honest *ha*! "*You're* gonna make a move on *Rachel*?"

Vern swallowed. His lips glistened with butter. "Yeah. Why not?"

Fitch sighed and watched Marsh sidle up to Rachel's friends. Marsh stood still, eyes focused on the screen, watching Rachel maneuver through the maze, eating pellets and chasing ghosts.

"Listen, *Henry*," Vern said. "Not all of us are as lucky in love as you and Big Bird."

A bolt of electricity shot through Fitch's arms. It happened that way sometimes, quick as lightning, and just as unexpected. Like lighting a match, except the match was deep in his bones. The spark made him want to grab Vern's shirt, twist it into a ball right under his throat, punch him in the stomach maybe, right where all that buttered popcorn now rested. Push him against one of the game cabinets—Defender or Asteroids, which were just a heartbeat away— and tell him, through clenched teeth, that if he made a comment like that again, Fitch would fix it to where he couldn't speak at all.

The fire blazed from his marrow to his skin, but instead of moving forward, Fitch forced his hands into his pockets and pushed his fists deep, deep, where they'd be safe.

"Good luck," Fitch said. Casual. Like the fire had never been. "I'm taking off. Let me know how it goes." He nodded toward Marsh. "Be careful, though. You've got competition."

GOOD NIGHT, BIRD

That night Bird lay in bed and wondered what it meant that being smart—not being pretty—was her "thing."

What about Judith Resnik? Jessica had said Judith Resnik was pretty, but she was also an astronaut, which meant she was smart. How could Jessica explain *that*?

Bird sighed. She always thought of good things to say when it was too late to actually say them.

Why did she care about being pretty, anyway? She didn't care in elementary school. She didn't even care that much last year. So why was she even thinking about it?

Bird knew that being pretty was important to her mother, even if Ms. Thomas liked to remind everyone that "looks don't matter." Was it important to everyone, then? Did Dani think about that kind of stuff? Ms. Salonga? Mission Specialist Judith Resnik?

Bird blinked at the ceiling. She created a picture in her mind of Judith Resnik fretting about her appearance as she gathered information about Halley's Comet. *Someone pass me the brush. I can't possibly do this kind of work with my hair like this.*

It didn't make sense.

Did it?

"I wish I could ask you," Bird whispered.

She closed her eyes. Formed a question. Imagined it traveling through the atmosphere, on the invisible waves of air from Delaware to Texas, and landing on Judith Resnik's ears.

Bird: It doesn't make sense to only be one thing. Does it?

And Judith's words, making the journey back.

Judith Resnik: No. It doesn't. Good night, Bird.

Bird: Good night.

HEY, AMANDA

"Well?" said Fitch, the moment Vern walked into first-period science.

Vern sailed down the aisle, smelling like sweat with a finger dab of cologne.

"Well, what?" he said.

Fitch turned in his desk as Vern sat down. "Did you talk to her?"

"Shh," Vern said, eyeing the front of the classroom, even though they both knew Rachel wasn't there yet.

"Did you?"

Vern unzipped his backpack and pulled out his science book. "Not exactly," he said. "I was going to, but your little friend wouldn't shut up."

"What little friend?"

"You know." Vern mimicked the way Marsh adjusted his glasses. "*Marsha* kept asking her questions and wouldn't shut up."

"Questions about what?"

"Ms. Pac-Man, of all things. *That's* what he was asking her about. Twenty questions per minute about Ms. Freaking *Pac-Man*. It was—" He stopped. His eyes drifted to the next aisle. The corners of his mouth turned upward.

Fitch knew what was coming.

"Oh, hey, Amanda," said Vern.

Fitch didn't look her way. Didn't move, even. But he heard her sit down, followed by the sounds of her arranging her books. He burrowed his eyes into Vern's face. A silent message: Don't you dare.

"I was just talking to Fitch—er, I mean *Henry*—about Ms. Pac-Man," said Vern.

"Oh, really?" Amanda smiled faintly. "I can never get past the first level."

"She's a tricky yellow ball," said Vern. He kicked his friend's foot with his sneaker. "Don't you think so, *Henry*?"

"Yeah," Fitch replied, voice flat. "Tricky."

"Do you ever go to the arcade on Main, Amanda?" Vern asked.

No. He wouldn't. Not even Vern would do such a thing. He would *not* invite Amanda Piper to hang out with them after school.

Would he?

Fitch's insides boiled.

He inhaled.

Deep breaths.

"Not really," said Amanda. "But when I go, I usually just play Q-Bert or something. I'm not good at that one either, though. Oh! I like Frogger. I can pass lots of levels on Frogger."

"Frogger," Vern repeated, nodding. "That's a good one. Right, Henry?"

Fitch was still sitting, his back to Amanda, glaring at Vern. If he moved, he might explode, like the Death Star in *Return of the Jedi* or the shark in *Jaws*. Every cell in his body was on edge. If Vern invited Amanda to the arcade, he wasn't sure what he'd do.

"Yeah," Fitch said, though he had already forgotten the question.

He wasn't able to move for a full three seconds, not until Andrea Blumenthal suddenly tapped Amanda on the shoulder to ask her something. With Amanda's attention occupied, Fitch whispered to Vern: "If you tell her to meet us at the arcade, you'll be my mortal enemy for life."

He was only half joking.

"Oh, please," said Vern. "I'm not stupid. I don't want Chewbacca there any more than you do. I have more important things to think about after school—like how I'm gonna turn myself into a white pellet for Ms. Pac-Man to gobble up." He raised his eyebrows toward Rachel Hill, who had just sauntered in, always the last to arrive.

Amanda showed up anyway. Fitch had forgotten all about the conversation and was standing next to Vern when he saw her. Vern was playing Joust and Fitch had lost all his quarters, so he was doomed to watch. Had he been playing Major Havoc, he might not have seen her and she may have been inclined to leave him alone—you can't really have a casual conversation with someone while they are in the middle of a game, after all; even Marsh knew that, and he was just a kid. But as luck would have it, Fitch happened to make eye contact with Amanda as she wandered past the claw machines.

Fitch muttered a swear word under his breath.

"What's wrong?" Vern asked, without looking at him.

"Amanda's here," he said, voice low.

Vern was down to one life, so he couldn't take his eyes away from the screen. Instead he scrunched his nose.

"Chewbacca?" he said.

Fitch had broken eye contact with Amanda the moment he'd made it, but she was walking toward them anyway.

This was all Vern's fault. He'd been mouthing off about the stupid arcade and now here she was. Why couldn't Vern ever shut up? With each step Amanda took, Fitch's skin warmed. She was smiling. Why was she always smiling at him? Didn't she get the hint?

"Hey, Henry," she said, waving.

Now she was standing next to him. She smelled like bubble gum, but she didn't appear to be chewing any.

"Hey, Vern," she added.

Vern mumbled "hey," too preoccupied to offer more. The digital sounds of Vern collecting eggs and flapping his Joust wings momentarily filled the air.

"This game looks so hard," Amanda said. "If it's called Joust, how come they aren't riding horses?" She and Fitch watched Vern flap, flap, flap. "Uh-oh! Watch out for that guy! Oh, no—look to your left!"

Fitch wanted to snap at her, tell her to be quiet, didn't she *know* you shouldn't roll up to someone in the middle of their game and tell them how to play, especially if you don't know how to play yourself? But he didn't need to because after Amanda's fourth "Watch out!" Vern's final ostrich died. He stepped back from the game console and lifted his arms in defeat, letting them fall to his sides with a smack.

"Great," Vern said. "Just great."

"Too bad," said Amanda. She had the nerve to look genuinely upset.

She shoved her hands in her pockets. "What're you gonna do now? Do you wanna try Skee-Ball?"

"Skee-Ball," said Vern, like she'd just suggested they write a research paper.

They never played the ticket games, like

Skee-Ball or air hockey. They were strictly *video gamers*. Didn't she know that?

Amanda pulled out a handful of coins. "I have quarters."

Fitch had an ugly thought right then: he imagined himself knocking the money out of her hand, scooping it up, and using all of it to play his own games.

"No thanks," Vern said. His eyes had locked onto something. Or more accurately, some*one*. Rachel Hill and her entourage—namely, Jessica Diaz and Jessica Brantley—were back at Ms. Pac-Man. Marsh, too.

Vern raked his hair with his fingertips.

"I didn't know Rachel came here, too," said Amanda.

There was a strange quality to her voice. Not jealousy, exactly. Fitch couldn't figure it out.

"Well, it's not like the two of you hang out," said Vern, chuckling.

Before she could respond, he told Fitch to

wish him luck and walked off. Fitch and Amanda stood there awkwardly, saying nothing. Amanda put the coins back in her pocket and Fitch watched Vern whisper something in Marsh's ear. The kid glanced their way and said something back to him—a question, it looked like—but Vern had already tuned him out and had practically nudged him out of the way.

Fitch's heart banged in his chest. He wanted Amanda to go away so he could resume his normal life, but she just kept standing there.

A group of boys came up to play Joust, so Fitch and Amanda inched over to make way. Marsh came toward them, ignoring other kids his age who yelled, "Marsha!" or "Marsha, Marsha, Marsha!" as he passed by.

"Hey," said Marsh, pushing up his glasses. "Your friend told me to come over here and rescue you, but I don't know what I'm rescuing you from." Marsh looked at Amanda. "Hey, I'm Marsh."

"Hey."

Fitch's heart thundered. *Whomp-whomp-whomp.*

"Your face is red, Henry," said Amanda.

And, as if that wasn't bad enough, she giggled.

At that moment, Fitch really hated her.

His mother said "hate" was a powerful and ugly word, only to be used when you really really meant it, "which shouldn't be often, if ever," she always added, but at that moment—at that very, very moment—Fitch really hated Amanda Piper. Why did she have to say his face was red? Why did anyone *ever* say that? He *knew* his face was red. Anyone could *see* his face was red, and now, because she'd opened her big mouth, his face was even redder.

He cleared his throat.

"See you two later," Fitch said.

Let the kid keep her company.

Fitch took an uneasy step away from them. He'd check the popcorn machine, that's what he'd do. At that moment, popcorn sounded like the most majestic food on the planet.

Fitch half expected Amanda to follow him, but Marsh did instead.

Fitch picked up his pace. All he'd wanted to do was hang out and play video games in peace. The arcade on Main was his *place*. His *only* place.

Fitch smelled the popcorn before he saw it—heaps and mountains, freshly popped. He grabbed an empty bag.

"I could eat a hundred bags of these," Marsh said, right behind him. He opened a bag, reached inside for the scooper, and filled it to the brim. Popcorn fell around his feet and collected there with dozens of other wayward pieces.

Mr. Hindley was passing by, holding a sack of coins in each hand. He nodded good-naturedly toward the floor on his way to the office.

"You missed some, Marsh," he said.

"I'm saving those for dessert, Mr. Hindley," Marsh replied.

Now here came Rachel Hill, walking ahead of the

Jessicas, ponytails bouncing on their shoulders.

"Hey," she chirped. She pointed to the popcorn machine. "We came for popcorn."

"Oh," Fitch said. He stepped aside.

"How'd you do on Ms. Pac-Man?" asked Marsh, his mouth full.

"Not so good today," Rachel replied. She shook open a bag and delicately scooped popcorn into it. Then she looked at Fitch and said, "Amanda's nice."

Fitch's brain skipped. He didn't understand what she was saying at first, or why she was saying it to him. *Amanda's nice?* What did that mean?

"Okay," he said. That's all his brain would allow. He suddenly felt very aware of every hair and sweat molecule on his body. Rachel and her friends seemed to be looking at him like they knew something he didn't.

"You make a cute couple," said Rachel. She smiled wide. A genuine, honest-to-goodness smile. A smile that showed that she meant what she was saying. She popped a kernel in her mouth. "Well, see you around!"

The girls turned on their heels and walked off chattering while Fitch stood fixed to his spot.

A cute couple?

A cute couple?

"Who's Amanda?" Marsh asked. He shoved another handful in his mouth. "Is that the girl you were standing with earlier?"

Fitch paused. Groaned inwardly. "Yes."

"I didn't know she was your girlfriend."

"She's not," said Fitch. "Don't you have friends your own age to hang out with?"

Marsh glanced toward the boys who'd called him Marsha. They were gathered around a claw machine.

Fitch walked off before Marsh could reply.

He kept hearing it, again and again.

You make a cute couple. You make a cute couple. You make a cute couple.

Really.

ALL IS FAIR

The cast itched. And it smelled. And it had "Penny L/S Charlie" written across it in permanent marker. In short: it was the greatest nightmare of Cash's life.

The urge to rip the whole thing off was almost unbearable, but he had no choice. He had to live with coat hangers and the smell of rotting fruit for the next few weeks.

But at least he had the game to look forward to. His father had ordered pizza, the cramped living room was designated a basketball-watching-only zone—meaning no one could come in, snatch the remote, and turn to something stupid like *Star Search* or *The Facts of Life*—and Dr. J and Charles Barkley were going to lead the team into a resounding victory over the Detroit Pistons.

Cash and his father settled into their places on the couch. Fitch was in his room, music up. Bird was flitting around the house, working on one of her new schematics. And Mrs. Thomas had cozied herself with a book on her bed, content to let everyone move in their own orbits.

It promised to be a decent night.

"Final score," said Cash's father, pointing at him with a tortilla chip. "Go. Best guess."

"One-twenty to one-fifteen," Cash said.

They did this every time they watched a game together. So far, neither of them had ever been right.

The first quarter ended with the Pistons ahead twenty-seven to fifteen. The tortilla chips were gone by the middle of the second. That's when

Bird emerged from the hallway with a notebook. She was already wearing her winter coat, hat, and gloves and had the front door halfway open when Mr. Thomas asked where she was going. He didn't take his eyes off Charles Barkley, who was moving in for a shot.

"Outside to look at constellations," Bird said.

When no one said anything, she walked outside and shut the door. The living room cooled momentarily from the blast of cold night air.

"Constellations," Mr. Thomas repeated, under his breath.

Cash didn't say anything. He, too, had been intrigued by Ms. Salonga's talk of stars and space, but the spark of interest had died as soon as he left the classroom. He certainly wasn't interested enough to sit outside in freezing weather with a notebook. Not that he could write much, anyway.

He picked up the coat hanger, shoved it in his cast, and scratched.

"Hey, uh . . . Dad?" he said. He cleared his

throat. Watching Dr. J with his father was one of his favorite things to do. It made him feel like they were on a team of their own. "Can I ask you something?"

Barkley missed a shot. Mr. Thomas cursed.

"Sure," said Mr. Thomas, eyes still on the game.

"Well . . ." Cash began. He arranged the words in his head. He'd thought about talking to Brant or Kenny, but no—it was too embarrassing. And now this felt embarrassing, too. "Uh . . . I don't know. Never mind."

"Come on, ask me."

"Well . . ." He paused. "There's this girl."

Mr. Thomas sat up. "Oh," he said. He turned down the volume and looked directly at Cash.

Eye contact is one of the simplest gifts you can give someone, Ms. Salonga once told Cash when he'd mumbled an answer—an incorrect answer, of course—to his notebook. *People need to feel seen.*

Cash suddenly felt like he was on display. With the TV turned down, the sound of Fitch's music blared down the hall.

"I mean," said Cash. "There's this girl at school. I don't know. I guess I kinda like her, maybe."

Mr. Thomas raised his eyebrows. "Yeah?"

"Yeah. But . . ." The back of his neck warmed with embarrassment. But the words were out there. Nothing to do about it.

"I think she likes this other guy."

"Is this guy a friend of yours?"

On TV, Moses Malone toed the foul line for a free throw.

Cash swallowed. "No. He's kind of . . ." Cash searched for an accurate word. Something his father would understand. ". . . a nerd, I guess."

"Hm." Mr. Thomas narrowed his eyes. "Let me tell you something, Cash. Your mom was the prettiest girl at Park High School back when we were kids. Popular. Funny. A cheerleader. At football games they'd put her up at the very top of the pyramid." He lifted an invisible cheerleader over his head. "Everyone would look at her, like 'Who's that girl?'"

Cash never knew that his mother had been at the top of the pyramid. He tried to imagine it, but the image wouldn't come together and he wasn't sure he wanted it to.

"I saw her and thought, I've got to get that girl. Problem was, every other guy was thinking the exact same thing. I had to come up with a strategy."

"What kind of strategy?"

"I figured I'd have to one-up all the other guys any way I could." He grinned. "All is fair in love and war, right?"

He put his hand out for Cash to slap in agreement, and Cash did, even though he wasn't totally sure what his father meant.

CHOOSE YOUR ADVENTURE

Fitch didn't like when he had to turn down his music. He kept the dial of his boom box on four—loud enough for him to feel like he was in his own music vacuum, but low enough that his parents didn't bang on the door and tell him to "turn it down" or "have some respect."

The sound of knocking had become an irritating itch to him. His hackles went up the minute he heard it. Like right now.

"What?" he yelled at the closed door.

He was sitting cross-legged on the floor next to the stereo, which blasted AC/DC as he read *Space and Beyond*, a Choose Your Own Adventure book Vern had let him borrow.

When Bird stuck her head in, he was on page twelve, trying to decide if he should fight the alien spacecraft outside his pod or go with them willingly. His instinct was to fight, but what if they were nice, innocent aliens?

Then again, what if they weren't?

Fitch turned down his music.

"Hey," Bird said. She had a notebook under her arm. "Wanna come outside and look at constellations with me?"

There was a time when they'd done many things together. Races to the end of the street. Hide-and-seek with just the two of them. Once they'd even tried to read each other's minds because they'd heard twins were supposed to be able to do that. They'd sat across from each other, squeezed their eyes shut, and communicated telepathically. Tried to, at least. Now Bird's mind was more foreign than it'd ever been. That bond they shared—that twin thing—had weakened somehow. Or maybe somewhen.

Fitch almost said yes.

He had thought about their mind-reading experience as recently as science class, when Ms. Salonga forced them to close their eyes and play make-believe space shuttle. Instead Fitch had thought about how he and Bird once sat just the same way, in chairs they'd pulled from the kitchen table, with their eyes closed, and Bird repeating, "Stop peeking, stop peeking."

But it was so cold outside.

And the nighttime was so quiet.

Too quiet.

"Nah," he said.

He turned the music up as Bird left the room.

He decided to fight the aliens, of course. He won the battle, but ultimately ended up floating in deep space with no chance of rescue. It wasn't really winning, in the end.

He tossed the book onto a heap of dirty clothes in the corner of his room. Maybe he *would* go outside to look at constellations. What else did he have to do?

He turned off his boom box, shoved his feet into his sneakers, and wandered into the living room. He expected to hear the loud cacophony of basketball, peppered with shouts from his father or brother, but they had the volume down and were talking quietly and slapping hands about something, as if they'd just made a business arrangement.

Fitch wondered what they were talking about.

"Where are you going?" Mr. Thomas asked.

Fitch pulled his coat from the rack and put it on. His dad had turned up the volume and was watching the game before Fitch answered, "Outside."

Bird was on the hood of the Cavalier, leaning back against the windshield. Her notebook was balanced on her legs, but she wasn't writing. Just staring up.

"Hey," Fitch said.

It was *cold.* Freezing, really. He climbed up next to her—carefully; if he made a dent in the car, he'd never hear the end of it—and leaned back, too. It was quiet, as suspected. The muffled sounds of the game came from the other side of the living room window, but it may as well have been in another galaxy.

The rest of the street was quiet, but lights glowed from living room and kitchen windows. Fitch wondered what all those other families were doing.

"You should get a blanket and lie in the backyard," Fitch said. "Then you wouldn't have to lie on the car."

Bird didn't say anything.

The stars were brighter than he expected. He couldn't remember the last time he'd looked at the sky for no reason whatsoever. Ms. Salonga said that many of the stars were bigger than the sun, but they looked minuscule from down here.

Fitch thought about his book. The aliens. Floating in deep space.

"Do you think there's life on other planets?" he asked. His breath puffed out of his mouth as he talked. It was strange to hear his voice without music or Major Havoc or other people pushing against it.

"Yeah," said Bird. "Do you?"

"Don't know."

"Maybe we'll find out someday. Someday soon." She paused. "Maybe *I'll* find out for us."

"How will you do that?"

"I'll become an astronaut like Judith Resnik and have NASA send me on a fact-finding mission."

"Judith who?"

Bird turned her head. "Judith Resnik. The mission specialist from *Challenger.*"

The name didn't sound familiar, but he could tell from Bird's tone that Judith Whatshername had been discussed in Ms. Salonga's class, which meant he was supposed to know who she was.

"But I won't be mission specialist," Bird continued, staring back at the sky. "I'll be the first female shuttle commander."

"Shuttle commander," Fitch repeated. "That sounds pretty cool."

"Yep. I'd be in charge of the whole ship."

Fitch suddenly felt very small under all the countless stars above them.

"I was in charge of my own space pod and I wound up floating in deep space after fighting a bunch of aliens who looked like amoebas," he said.

"Is that from a video game or something?"

"No. *Space and Beyond.* Choose Your Own Adventure."

His nose felt like a tiny block of ice. His fingertips were numb.

"Aren't you cold?" he asked.

"A little, but I'm wearing a hat and gloves," she said. "If you want to stay warm, you have to cover the areas where heat escapes, like your head, hands, and feet. It's just basic science."

Fitch sat up. He was wearing neither a hat nor gloves. "I'm cold. I'm gonna go back in."

"Okay," Bird said.

Fitch slid off the car. It groaned under his weight, but no real damage was done.

"Don't get abducted by aliens," he said. When he reached the front door, he turned and said, "And if you do, don't leave without me."

THE MOST INCREDIBLE MACHINE OF ALL

Later that night Fitch gave Bird one of his old cassettes. He said he never listened to it anymore.

"May as well donate its body to science," he said, cradling the tape in the palms of his hands as if it were a dead mouse.

She placed it under the lamp on her desk, next to an ever-growing pile of *Bird's-Eye Views*.

"Why do you do this stuff? It seems so boring," Fitch said, not unkindly, as he flicked the drawing with his thumb.

Bird balanced a tiny screwdriver on the uppermost corner of his tape, which she now saw was the soundtrack to *Rocky*. It brought back a distinct memory, long forgotten, of her parents arguing. She, Cash, and Fitch were dressed for the movies because they were supposed to see *Rocky IV*. The movie was scheduled to start at one p.m., but their parents argued until long after that, and by the time the house rested back into silence, everyone had disappeared into their own orbits. They never made it to the theater at all. Bird still hadn't seen it, but Devonte said it was stupid, so she figured she hadn't missed much.

The original *Rocky* had once been Fitch's favorite movie. Bird wondered if it still was.

"I don't know," she said. "The same reason you play video games."

"Video games are fun. But this?" He scrunched his nose. "This is like homework."

Bird shrugged and turned the tiny screwdriver

counterclockwise—slowly, slowly. It was easy for machines to lose their parts, especially tiny ones like this. The smallest pieces could make the biggest difference.

"I guess I just like to see how things work," she said.

"I already know how a cassette tape works. You put it in and hit Play." He walked toward the door.

"Don't you wanna see the inside of your tape?" Bird asked.

"Nah. You can show me later."

Oh, well. Maybe it was for the best that she was working alone again. It gave her time to think. The sounds of the basketball game and her brother's boom box slipped away as she studied the components of the cassette and sketched her newest schematic.

The mind was the most incredible machine of all, she thought, because it did so many things at once. At this moment, for instance, Bird was sketching the interior mechanisms of a cassette tape, thinking about Halley's Comet, and doing math simultaneously. By her calculations, after this year, Halley's Comet wouldn't appear again until 2061 and then 2134. She could hardly imagine the year 2000—a new millennium!— much less the years 2061 or 2134.

Bird: What do you think Halley's Comet will look like from the *Challenger*?

Judith Resnik: I don't know. Spectacular, probably.

Bird: Everything looks spectacular from a space shuttle, I bet.

Judith Resnik: That's true.

Bird: What's it like, anyway?

Judith Resnik: It's like being far away and close at the same time. Floating in a world that belongs only to you, but also belongs to everyone else.

Bird: That doesn't make much sense.

Judith Resnik: True. But neither does life on Earth.

Bird: You're right. It makes less sense every year. Sometimes I feel like I have a million questions, but I don't know what most of them are. And I have no one to ask.

Judith Resnik: You can ask me.

Bird: Well . . .

Judith Resnik: Don't worry. I won't tell anyone.

Bird: A girl at school said being pretty isn't my

thing. She says being smart is my thing. I already know I'm smart.

Judith Resnik: So, what's your question?

Bird: Am I pretty?

Judith Resnik: In my opinion, being smart *is* pretty.

Bird: That's not really an answer.

Judith Resnik: Maybe. But to be honest, it's an unanswerable question.

Bird: Why is it unanswerable?

Judith Resnik: Because there is no pretty.

Bird: That's not true. There's a girl at my school, Rachel. Everyone thinks she's pretty.

Judith Resnik: Okay. Then who's prettier—Rachel or Dani?

Bird: That's impossible to say. They look nothing alike.

Judith Resnik: Exactly. "Pretty" isn't real, Bird. It's one person looking at another and saying yes or no, based on their own personal judgments. And it's transient. It's like the wind—society says something is pretty one minute, then they decide it's not pretty anymore, and everyone moves where it takes them. Pretty is nothing. Pretty is invisible. Pretty is what you make it.

Bird repeated that phrase in her mind: *Pretty is nothing. Pretty is invisible. Pretty is what you make it.*

Maybe if she said it enough times, she could wish it into being.

BIRD'S-EYE VIEW:
CASSETTE TAPE

EXTERIOR

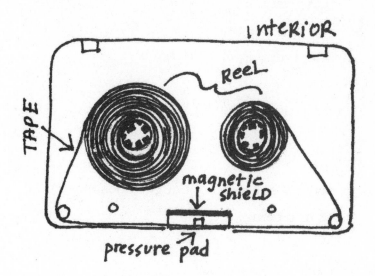

Gonna Fly Now · Philadelphia Morning ·
Going the Distance · Reflections ·
Marines Hymn · Take You Back ·
First Date

ROCKY
ORIGINAL SOUNDTRACK

1

INTERIOR

REEL

TAPE

magnetic
shield

pressure pad

GREAT WAY
TO START THE DAY

The morning had not started well. Maybe it was an omen.

Fitch had overslept, for one thing. He woke up with *Space and Beyond* under his head, its cover creased and folded, the last paragraph— *Maybe you can start all over. Maybe you can rematerialize. Try it.*—inching into his brain as the alarm buzzed.

When he opened his eyes, his first thought was: *I don't want to go to school.* This was often his first thought, but today it ran through his mind like a mantra, and he lay there for twenty extra minutes. He listened to everyone else moving around the house, knowing that sooner or later his mother would call his name and the sound would grate him to the bone.

He was right.

"Fitch! *FITCH!*"

He wanted to fake sick. Complain of a headache, stomachache, anything. But then he'd have to deal with his parents. They'd be suspicious. If one said yes and the other didn't, it would turn into a big thing.

It wasn't worth it.

He got ready in a hurry, but it wasn't fast enough for his parents, of course.

"It's really inconsiderate to keep everyone waiting, Fitch," his mother said, as they all zipped their winter coats. "The whole world doesn't revolve around you, you know."

"What difference does it make?" said Fitch. "Dad's the one who drops us off."

"That's not the point."

Mr. Thomas opened the front door. A gust of cold wind came into the house. Cash and Bird went out, quickly.

"The point is, you're very inconsiderate. You only think about yourself."

"We don't have time for this, Tam," his father said, keys in hand.

Mrs. Thomas was slipping on a glove. She stopped halfway. "Time for what, exactly?" she said.

"Whatever this is," his father said.

Fitch stepped outside and moved quickly toward the car, where Bird and Cash were waiting. A few houses down, one of the neighbor girls—her last name was Riley; Fitch couldn't remember her first—was walking out the door with her parents. The girl was in fourth or fifth grade. Fitch hoped his parents' argument didn't carry itself outside. It wouldn't be the first time.

"It would be *nice* if you backed me up once

in a while with the kids, you know," his mother said. She yanked the second glove out of her pocket and put it on. "I don't need you correcting me in front of them."

She closed the front door and locked it behind her.

"Oh, right, right," said Mr. Thomas, walking toward the Cavalier. "You're the perfect parent. I forgot." He shoved the key into the driver's door. The lock popped up at the same time he muttered something under his breath. A colorful name for their mother, Fitch presumed.

"Great way to start the day, Mike!" his mother called, as she unlocked her own car. "Real mature!"

Cash, Fitch, and Bird couldn't get inside the car fast enough. Cash took the passenger seat— he always got to sit in the front, somehow— while Bird and Fitch slipped into the back. Fitch watched the Riley girl get into her mother's car. He wondered what life was like at the Rileys'.

He'd mowed the grass for them a few times last summer. Mrs. Riley gave him an extra five dollars.

"You kids should start taking the bus in the morning," their father said, after a few minutes of silence. "It stops right on the corner."

Fitch looked out the window.

"I wouldn't mind," Bird said. "It could be—"

"No way," said Cash. "The bus comes at, like, seven in the morning. I don't wanna be standing on the corner at seven in the morning."

"I wouldn't mind," Bird repeated, more quietly this time.

Fitch didn't have an opinion. There was no escaping school, so what difference did it make if they took a car or a bus?

Once they got dropped off, Fitch went straight to his locker and Vern appeared in minutes, waggling his eyebrows and grinning stupidly.

"Guess what?" Vern said, leaning against the row of lockers as Fitch arranged his things.

"What? You grow a second head over the weekend or something?"

Vern moved his head from left to right. "Not that I can tell. But I *did* talk to Rachel Hill on the phone yesterday."

"How did that happen?" said Fitch. "She dial the wrong number?"

"Ha. Ha. Very funny, jerk-wad."

Fitch moved between his locker and the mess of his backpack. As Vern babbled on, a secret wish formed in the bottom of Fitch's mind and rose to the surface. A wish that his locker would crack open and transport him somewhere. Like a portal. Make him Vader in the *Death Star*. Luke in the desert, even. Just put him anywhere but Park Middle School listening to Vern.

Fitch tossed his backpack over his shoulder and nodded at all the right times as Vern talked and talked. His irritation took root and sprouted.

Maybe it was the way Vern had walked up, all smug, like he'd accomplished some big feat.

Maybe it was the way Vern never shut up.

Maybe it was the way his mother had called him "inconsiderate" that morning.

"So, what'd you do this weekend?" Vern finally asked.

"Not much," Fitch mumbled, which was the truth, although he'd had a peak moment yesterday afternoon when he'd discovered two quarters in the couch and three under a stack of old copies of the *News Journal.*

Why couldn't life be like a VCR, with rewind and fast-forward buttons? He'd fast-forward this day directly to the arcade. Presuming Amanda wouldn't be there.

And speaking of.

"Hey, Vern. Hey, Henry." She smiled and half waved as she sat down. She looked different today, but Fitch couldn't figure out why and he didn't want to spend too much time studying her face for an answer. "Did you have a good weekend?" she asked.

He decided to ignore the question. Let Vern answer, since he was such a ladies' man.

"I certainly did," said Vern. "What about you, Henry?"

Vern kicked the back of his chair.

Fitch bounced his knee up and down, up and down.

Andrea Blumenthal, who sat in front of Amanda, glanced between him and Amanda and smiled knowingly. It was a smile like Rachel's. Fitch could practically read her thoughts. *You make a cute couple.*

He mumbled something like "yes."

This "Henry" thing was getting out of hand. It really was.

An angry buzzing pulsed under his skin.

"My weekend was okay," said Amanda, though no one had asked. And now she launched into a breathless description of all she'd done—she went to the mall with her mother, she bought new sneakers, she rented movies—as Fitch faced forward, suddenly mesmerized by Ms. Salonga standing at the classroom door, his knee bouncing up and down and up and down, his skin buzzing, beads of sweat pushing their way out of his neck. He couldn't really hear anything Amanda was saying, but one word rang like a bell and set his fingertips on fire. *Henry, Henry, Henry.*

" . . . do you like movies, Henry? . . . what kind, Henry? . . . what do you think, Henry?"

It was the last "Henry," the final "Henry" right before the tardy bell, that set him off. Flicked a switch. Set fire to every cell in his body. He shot out of his chair with so much force that his desk shook and wobbled out of place, and he faced her, this Amanda, this girl who had ruined his mornings and now his afternoons, this girl with her round, ruddy cheeks and her big hair, this girl who just *had* to talk about his red face, who played Skee-Ball and gave him stickers, and he realized now why she looked different—she was wearing makeup, *makeup.* His red cheeks blazed. He clenched his fists at his sides, took a quick, deep breath, and yelled, with all the rage firing through his body: "My name is Fitch, you FAT, STUPID COW! *Fitch!* If we're calling each other by our real names, I guess I should call *you* Chewbacca!"

A piece of spittle flew out of his mouth and rested on his chin. He picked up his notebook, the one with the TIE fighter doodle that started it all, and hurled it across the room. It hit one of Ms. Salonga's bookcases, fluttered open like a butterfly, then fell facedown. Someone screamed—a short, quick scream of shock—and then the bell rang and everything was silent, as if he'd stepped into a deep void in space. Someone laughed. And they were all laughing at what Fitch had said and done, which made him even angrier. It was a terrible thing, to laugh at someone else's expense. But he was the one who'd put the words out there in the first place.

Amanda's face was a mess of circles. Wide eyes, mouth like an O. She looked frozen, like she was in the middle of a game of freeze tag. But then she moved. Her eyes sparkled under their new shades of blue. But no, they weren't sparkling. They were wet. Pooling. And her bottom lip trembled.

Ms. Salonga's voice drifted into his brain from faraway.

"Fitch Thomas," she said. "In the hall. Now."

But it was Amanda who left the room—quickly, in big, awkward steps. She moved clumsily. She stumbled. Her foot slid on Fitch's splayed notebook and she wobbled, her arms in the air, like a character in a cartoon, and the whole room held its breath as she slipped and fell. Someone made a noise—a wrangled gasp; maybe the noise came from Amanda, it was hard to tell—and then her rounded arms were in the air again as she struggled to stand. Ms. Salonga reached out to help her, but Amanda didn't clutch the teacher's hands. Instead she used the bookcase for leverage and finally she was up and out of the room. Ms. Salonga took a step in her direction, but before she did, she leveled her eyes at Fitch, and he knew—right then and there—that he would remember that look for the rest of his life.

Ms. Salonga often talked about the importance of eye contact.

People need to feel seen, she always said.

He was silent and still.

Everyone was.

No one was laughing anymore.

No one breathed at all.

ONE-UP

All is fair in love and war. No rules. Survival of the fittest.

It was time to do some one-upping. Show

Penny why she should L/S Cash Nelson Thomas instead of Charlie Whatever.

There was a problem, though.

Cash couldn't one-up anything.

Let's face it. Charlie was an honors student. Sure, he was probably terrible at sports, but what difference did that make? Cash wasn't exactly Moses Malone, either.

What, then?

He'd have to go with his instincts.

Luckily, Ms. Salonga provided the perfect opportunity.

Truth be told, Cash didn't pay attention to anything she said until she got to this part: "I want you to pair off," said Ms. Salonga. "One of you take out a sheet of paper and draw a vertical line down the middle—remember, vertical is up and down; horizontal is across—and on one side, write 'Humans' at the top. On the other side write 'Machines.' Under each column, write a list of pros and cons for each." She demonstrated on the board. "In what ways are humans better than machines and vice versa? What are the benefits of one versus the other? Think of as many examples as you can."

Penny turned her desk completely around to face him and when she sat down and smiled, his stomach dropped. For a fleeting moment, he thought he might throw up.

Penny took out a clean sheet of paper and did as instructed. She dotted her *i* in "Machines" with a perfect round circle.

"I can think of a few already," she said. Under "Machine," she wrote "more logical." "What about you?"

Cash stared at the paper. "Uh," he said. "Machines are . . . more reliable, I guess?"

Penny shook her head. "I think people are more reliable. Machines break down all the time."

"Oh." Cash shrugged. "Yeah. You're probably right."

She wrote "more reliable" under "Humans."

"Humans . . . uh . . . they know what they're doing. Like, they can look at a situation from all sides. So they don't make as many mistakes, maybe," Cash said. "Machines can make mistakes."

Penny shook her head again. "No. It's the other way around. Humans make mistakes. Machines *never* make mistakes."

"Oh," Cash said.

She wrote "never make mistakes" under "Machines."

"So . . ." Cash said as she made another perfect circle over her *i*. "What'd you do this weekend?"

"I saw a movie with my parents. *The Money Pit.*"

"Was it good?"

"It was pretty funny, I guess. I wanted to see *April Fool's Day*, but my parents wouldn't let me." She tapped her pencil against the paper and stared at something above his head, apparently lost in thought. Was she actually trying to focus on this assignment?

"Did Charlie go, too?" Casual, casual.

"Charlie? Oh. No."

"How long have you been going together, anyway?"

She looked at him and smiled. "We have our two-month anniversary next week."

Two months.

That was a lot longer than Cash thought.

He wondered if they'd kissed yet.

He had almost kissed Stephanie Browne last year. They'd sat side by side through a whole basketball game, then they walked to the concession stand together. On the way there, they slipped out the side door because Stephanie said the gym was stuffy and smelled like feet. Once they were out of sight, he leaned forward to kiss her, but she suddenly stepped back and said she wanted to go back inside. Her cheeks turned bright, bright red, but he didn't say anything. To be honest, he was partly relieved. His stomach had been in knots.

But now he was the only one of his friends

who hadn't kissed anyone. Brant had kissed Julianne Whatley the summer before sixth grade, and Kenny had gone with Rachel Hill for three months in seventh. They were passing him in everything, it seemed, and it would get even worse as time pushed on. Next year they'd be in high school, and where would he be? Sitting in a desk at Park Middle School, that's where.

"He's kind of a dork, don't you think?" Cash said.

It came out unexpectedly. Like his brain had lost control of his mouth. He wasn't even sure he thought Charlie *was* a dork. Maybe he was. But Cash never expected to say something like that to Penny.

Penny blinked at him. "What do you mean?"

Cash put his arms under his desk. He didn't want her to get a whiff of the disgusting sweat smell emanating from his cast.

"I'm just saying. He's a dork. I'm surprised you're going with him."

He couldn't one-up Charlie in anything, but he certainly could drag him down low enough for Penny to see the error of her ways.

All is fair in love and—

"I like him," Penny said. Her mouth was a tight line. "I don't care if someone like *you* thinks he's a dork or not."

Someone like you.

What did that mean?

He wasn't sure what he thought she'd say, but it wasn't that.

"Whatever," he said. "I don't care who you go with, to be honest." He leaned back in his desk and raised his hand. Time to abort mission by any means necessary. "Ms. Salonga, can I go to the bathroom?"

Ms. Salonga looked up from Craig Baker's desk, where she was answering questions. "Can you wait until after class? I'd prefer if you finished the assignment."

"We're almost done anyway, Ms. Salonga,"

said Penny. Her voice was strained. Annoyed.

Ms. Salonga sighed. "Fine. But come right back."

He didn't come right back. Once he was in the hallway, he realized how desperate he was to be somewhere else. He hated school. He tried not to use that word often—his mother discouraged it, something about hate being ugly and it was, of course it was—but there was no better word for it. He felt more at home in the empty halls, where he had space to breathe. Out here, roaming free, felt surreal. Like a secret just for him. All the lockers were shut. No squeaking sneakers except for his high-tops.

He moved slowly to the bathroom even though he didn't need to go. When he got there, he walked in and out with every intention of meandering back to class. But his feet turned in the opposite direction. Where was he going? He had no idea.

He paused near the trophy cases. The basketball team had won a championship the previous year, after he'd been dropped.

Too bad they didn't give trophies for being able to run across the court without sinking any shots. He would've gotten the tallest one.

There were also trophies for spelling bees, academics, and quiz bowls. There were black-and-white photos of kids who placed first in the state science fair. Cash squinted at their faces and wondered what it was like to be someone who willingly participated in academic activities. It was hard to imagine—almost as impossible as his mother on top of a pyramid.

When a door opened down the hall, he acted like he was going to the bathroom again. After walking a few steps in that direction, he realized no one was behind him so he lingered, trying to figure out his next move.

Ah, the water fountain. Good idea. He stepped toward it, still taking his time, and pushed the button. He even leaned down like he was taking big, huge gulps, but actually he was letting the water make its weak arc and fall back into the drain. He never drank from the water fountains unless he had to. It was disgusting. Like swallowing a mouthful of pennies.

Okay. Now what?

He wandered away from the fountain, away from Ms. Salonga's classroom, away from her imaginary space shuttles and vertical lists. His feet, still working independently from his body, led him to the school's front entrance.

What if he just walked off?

Just—left?

What if he went across the street and didn't come back until class was over? It was freezing outside, but he could stand it for twenty minutes or so, right? What if he ran? Anything was better than being in that classroom. He could run around the block a few times, get some fresh air, and hurry back when the bell rang.

"Sorry, Ms. Salonga," he'd say. "I had a really upset stomach."

She probably hadn't even noticed he was gone.

He stared at the door like a prisoner dreaming of freedom. He was at the cusp of making a decision—at least, he thought he was—when he realized that his mom's car was parked outside, in the circle where they did drop-offs and pickups.

But that didn't make any sense.

He took a tentative step forward and narrowed his eyes, like he was looking at a mirage.

It was definitely his mom's car. There was the dent from the time Fitch accidentally rammed his wagon into the bumper years ago, and there was the Strawberry Shortcake sticker Bird had pressed into the back window when she was in first or second grade.

But why was the car here now?

Was there an event today? Was that why his mom was there? He racked his brain. No. It was just an ordinary Monday.

Fitch or Bird must be sick. They'd both looked

fine that morning, but who can tell? If it was Fitch, he was probably faking.

Maybe he should get fake-sick, too.

Maybe he was feeling sick *right now.*

He cradled his stomach, putting on a show with no audience as he made his way to the bathroom yet again. Once inside, he went into a stall, leaned against one of the walls, and stood there. He wanted to sit, but the toilets had no lids.

He would've stayed there until he couldn't stand it any longer, but the door opened about five minutes later and someone said his name.

It was Craig, from Ms. Salonga's class.

"You in here?" Craig said.

Cash paused. He felt really stupid now, standing inside a locked stall.

"Yeah," he said.

"Ms. Salonga made me come get you," said Craig. He seemed embarrassed, too.

"I'm coming."

"Cool."

The door closed. Cash sighed. But he had made an executive decision: he would tell Ms. Salonga he was sick. Maybe he had the stomach flu. The stomach was always the perfect culprit. It was hard to fake a sore throat, runny nose, or fever. But a stomachache? A few moans and groans, big deal.

Mom was already here. What difference did it make?

By the time he walked back into the classroom, he had the entire day planned out—junk food on the couch, watch a movie. His dad had rented *Rambo* over the weekend, and it was still sitting on top of the VCR.

Everyone was putting their desks back in their original positions when the bell rang and Ms. Salonga waved him over. He made sure to walk like someone with severe stomach pains. As soon as he reached her desk, he planned to ask for an office pass, but the words disappeared when she started talking.

"You skipped half the class," she said.

Maybe she'd been paying attention after all.

Cash didn't say anything. What could he say? She'd made a statement, not a question.

He formed a series of words in response. *I'm not feeling well, Ms. Salonga. I need to . . .*

"You haven't been turning in all your assignments," Ms. Salonga said. She locked eyes with him and raised her eyebrows. "And your grade is slipping."

Assignments and grades. That's all teachers cared about. Seriously. Didn't they have *lives*? Were the grades of Cash Nelson Thomas of such importance to her that she just *had* to get to the bottom of it?

"My grade was already low to begin with, so . . ." He didn't know how to finish the sentence.

"You have a passing grade, Cash," she said. "But you're getting close to a D. And you seem distracted." She paused. "Is everything okay?"

Students from her next-period class trickled in. Brant's younger sister, Jessica, and her best friend, who was also named Jessica. He couldn't remember her last name. Diaz, maybe? She smiled at him. He nodded back, then turned to Ms. Salonga.

"It's been hard to do homework and stuff with my cast and everything," Cash said.

His feet itched to run.

"I don't mean your cast." She lowered her voice. "Listen. Please know you can always come to me if you need anything."

Oh god.

This was the most embarrassing moment of his life.

"Okay," Cash mumbled.

More students were coming in.

As if things couldn't get worse, Bird was walking through the door. She gave him a quizzical look on her way to her desk.

"That's all, Cash," Ms. Salonga said.

He beelined for the door.

IF BROTHERS WERE MACHINES

Bird and Cash had nothing in common. He was a mystery to her. They came from the same parents and lived in the same house, but he was a puzzle. She could put the pieces together but didn't understand the picture. If he were a machine, he would be something simple with unreliable output, like a dot-matrix printer that always ran out of ink.

If Fitch were a machine, he'd be something hot that sparks.

"Bird, did you hear about your brother?" Jessica Brantley, aka JB, stage-whispered as they all settled into their desks for science.

Dani, Devonte, and other kids wandered in.

Bird glanced toward Ms. Salonga, who was greeting the third-period class.

"Who? Cash?" Bird asked, glancing toward the door that her brother had just exited.

Jessica Diaz picked up the conversational baton.

"He totally *lost it* this morning," she said. "He went *ballistic* on Amanda Piper in front of everyone. He called her a cow or something. I heard they had to call the *police.*"

Fitch.

"They didn't call the police," said Dani, rolling her eyes as she unzipped her backpack. "They just sent him to the principal's office."

Devonte turned around. "Who went to the principal's office?"

"Bird's brother, Fitch," JB said, flipping her blond hair. "He went crazy in class. This class. Ms. Salonga. First period."

"But . . . why?" Bird said.

"Who cares?" Jessica Diaz said. "No one deserves to be called a fat cow in front of the whole school."

"I heard she called him a name first," Other Jessica said.

"What did she call him?" Bird asked.

The Jessicas shrugged.

Bird had more questions—about a hundred more—but the tardy bell ended their conversation. Ms. Salonga launched directly into the lesson without missing a beat. Bird studied her face for any hint of something terrible happening just two hours earlier, but she looked like her usual self.

"The *Challenger* mission at the end of this month is possible because of the extraordinary abilities of humans and machines," Ms. Salonga said. "Obviously, we *build* machines to accomplish things that we can't, or to make a process more efficient. There is a lot of discourse over whether this will be to our detriment or not. That's a conversation that's been happening since the Industrial Age. . . . Yes, Christopher?"

"What's discourse?"

Ms. Salonga pulled the dictionary from her bookshelf and continued talking. "Without humans advancing technology, things like telephones,

VCRs, and stereos wouldn't be possible. Certainly, we wouldn't be able to launch a shuttle into space!" She placed the dictionary on Christopher's desk. "But just as there are things that humans can't do, there are many ways in which machines fall short. This will be our focus for the first half of the period. I want you to get together with your pair partner and come up with two lists."

Desks were already being moved, including Devonte's.

"I want you to divide your paper vertically down the middle," Ms. Salonga said. "On one side, I want you to—yes, Jessica?"

"Is vertical across or up and down?" Jessica Diaz asked.

"Up and down," continued Ms. Salonga. "On one side I want you to write 'Humans,' and on the other, write 'Machines.' Then you and your partner will discuss ways in which one is better, or worse, than the other. Kind of like a pros and cons list."

When Devonte and Bird were facing each other, Devonte leaned forward and said, "Sorry about your brother, Bird."

She didn't feel like smiling, but she did anyway.

"I'm sure there's an explanation," she said, though she wasn't sure at all.

She thought about Amanda Piper. Amanda was tall and awkward and didn't have many friends. Some of the kids called her names. Including Fitch, apparently. Bird had never spoken to her, but she seemed nice. She certainly didn't seem like someone who deserved to be called a fat cow.

Then again, who did?

Bird waited until everyone else had turned in their assignments before she approached Ms. Salonga's desk with the list she'd completed with Devonte.

"Ms. Salonga," Bird said, quietly. "Can I ask you something?"

"About the assignment or something else?" Ms. Salonga said.

"Um. Something else."

Ms. Salonga brought Bird into the hall. It was strange to stand on the other side of the door, alone with a teacher in gaping silence. The class watched with curious eyes, as they always did when someone was singled out for something mysterious, like a private hallway conference with the teacher.

"Is everything okay?" Ms. Salonga asked. She was wearing one of her banana clips today, and her lips were pink. Bird imagined Ms. Salonga teaching *her* how to use a banana clip and put on makeup. It was a sudden, strange thought.

A four-foot cardboard cutout of the space shuttle was on the wall between Ms. Salonga's door and the lockers. Bird absently pressed a wayward square of tape with her index finger.

"Someone said something about my brother . . ." Bird began. "About your class."

Ms. Salonga nodded. She didn't seem surprised.

"Fitch, I mean," said Bird. "I heard he yelled at someone . . . I don't know. And they had to call the police."

"The police!" Ms. Salonga shook her head. "No one called the police. Your brother was sent to the office this morning after an outburst. That's all."

"Oh." Bird nodded. She moved onto another square of tape.

"Is everything okay, Bird?" Ms. Salonga said. "At home, I mean? Or in general?"

"Yeah. I just wanted to make sure Fitch was okay. And . . . you know, whoever else was involved." Bird thought of Amanda.

Ms. Salonga inhaled. "And what about you? How are you?"

Bird shrugged with one shoulder. "I'm fine. I'm worried about my brothers. Not just Fitch, but Cash, too. I don't want him to fail seventh grade again, and I—"

"I understand all that, Bird," Ms. Salonga said, gently. "But I asked about *you*. How are *you*?"

"Oh." Bird dropped her hand from the wall. "I'm fine."

She didn't feel like smiling.

But she did.

HUMANS	MACHINES
— more adaptable	— more Reliable
— too emotional	— objective
— makes mistakes	— very logical
— unpredictable	— doesn't get tired
	— doesn't complain
	— stronger
	— works faster
	— never makes mistakes
	— you always know what will happen.

— BIRD THOMAS
— Devonte HARRiS

IF, THEN

If he'd stayed home from school, then none of this would have happened.

If Amanda had called him by the right name, then he never would have popped off.

If Vern hadn't annoyed him with his endless chatter, then maybe he wouldn't have been in such a terrible mood.

If, then. If, then.

You could *if, then* for the rest of your life, but it didn't change *now*. And right now, here he was, sitting across from his mother in the living room. He couldn't remember the last time it was just the two of them. According to the clock above the television, he should be sauntering into third period, ticking off the minutes until dismissal. Instead he was trapped on the couch with his mother—who wanted to "have a talk"—and the wayward stacks of junk mail that were never put away.

Let's hear it, Fitch thought. *Let's hear how inconsiderate I am.*

Here's the funny thing, though: he knew he was in the wrong. He *knew* how cruel he'd been. But he was still angry. Not at himself, not at Vern, not even at Amanda Piper. At this moment, he was angry at his mother. He didn't understand why. Maybe it was the way she was sitting here, leveling him with a look of utter disappointment on every inch of her face.

"I don't understand what's gotten into you," she said. "How could you do that to someone? You had such a big heart when you were a kid. I'm completely baffled."

Fitch focused on the scattered mail next to his mother. Some of the threads were loose in the couch cushion.

"You know we don't condone that kind of talk," she continued.

Fitch's mind ticked backward to that very morning. *Great way to start the day, Mike! Real mature!* And the word his father had used when he unlocked the car door.

Grown-ups were such hypocrites.

He wanted to say that, wanted to say it right out loud, but he suddenly felt like one huge cement block. Unable to speak or move. Let her think what she wanted. He knew the truth. He wouldn't speak a single word. Not a word. What difference did it make?

"Don't imagine for one second that you're spending any time at the arcade while you're out of school," she said.

He'd been suspended for three days. The first time any of the Nelson Thomas children had been suspended, his mother made sure to point out. As if he didn't already know that.

His parents had a habit of pointing out things that he already knew.

His mother leaned forward, bowed her head, and rubbed her temples. "You boys cause so much stress. I need a vacation."

Fitch thought of his locker. How he'd wished it would turn into a portal and carry him off somewhere.

"Are you done?" he said. "I wanna go to my room."

Seconds passed. She didn't look up.

"Go," she finally said.

So he did.

CHEERS

When Dani Logan asked her to stay for dinner, Bird didn't know what to expect. Would everyone serve themselves in the kitchen and go their separate ways, like at home? Bird didn't think so. Maybe because the dining room table was clean and clear. Or maybe it was the way Dani's parents cooked together.

Dinner was meat loaf and mashed potatoes. After preparing a modest plate, Bird followed Dani to the table. The girls sat on one side; Mr. and Mrs. Logan sat on the other. Dani's mother was small and round—the kind of figure Ms. Nelson Thomas feared above all else. Mr. Logan had an angular nose like Dani.

"We just hired this new guy and I have to train him," Mr. Logan said, as he mashed his tower of potatoes with a fork. "I'm pretty sure he's more confused than ever now. My training is all over the place. One minute I'm talking about processing, the next minute I'm showing him the fax machine. Poor guy."

Bird swallowed a small bite of food, then said, "You should make a list."

"A list?"

"Yeah, like a training to-do list. Then you can keep track of what you've already covered and what you need to do next."

Mr. Logan smiled. "That's a great idea." He tapped his fork against his water glass. *Clink, clink.* "Hear ye, hear ye. Starting tomorrow I will make a list."

Bird smiled. It had been a long time since a grown-up told her she had a great idea. Who was the last person? Ms. Salonga, probably.

What a strange universe, Bird thought. She felt silly admitting this—even to herself—but she didn't know families really ate dinner together. Sure, Ms. Salonga had told them stories of how her family ate together, and how they had rules, like no arguing at the table. But it still seemed like a fairy tale; something that only existed in tall tales or on TV.

"Dani told us all about you, Bernadette," Mrs. Logan said. She wiped her mouth with a napkin and smiled. "She says you're very smart."

"Everyone calls her Bird," said Dani. "And she's one of the smartest kids at school."

Bird's cheeks warmed. She felt shy and proud all at once.

"Good thing she's on your space team then," Mr. Logan said. "You don't want to get to the comet and have no idea what to do next."

Bird was about to politely explain that they were crews, not space teams, but something moved in the corner of her eye and she turned, hoping to get a glance of the elusive Chekov.

No such luck.

"Bird wants to be a real shuttle commander when she grows up," said Dani.

"Really?" Mrs. Logan said. "How exciting."

"What's a shuttle commander do?" asked Mr. Logan.

"They're in charge of the whole ship," Dani replied.

"NASA has never had a female shuttle commander before," Bird said. "I want to be the first one."

"You'll be the next Sally Ride!" Mrs. Logan said.

Bird smiled. "Or the next Judith Resnik,

mission specialist on the space shuttle *Challenger.*"

Mr. Logan lifted his glass, followed by Mrs. Logan and the girls.

"To the next Judith Resnik!" he said.

They all tapped their glasses together. *Clink, clink.* Cheers.

ONE HUNDRED?

"Dude, you know what I realized in math class today?" said Kenny.

Cash was sitting on the concrete with his arms resting on his knees, watching Brant's pathetic attempts at Hacky Sack. Kenny was next to him, also eyeing Brant, and occasionally providing helpful commentary—"You're seriously the worst at this, Brant," and "You're a disgrace" being the most common critiques. Their friendship seemed built on personal failures.

"That you don't know how to add or subtract?" said Brant, his voice breathy from lifting his ankles and knees, desperate to keep the Hacky Sack in play. Brant's winter jacket hindered his movements, making it difficult for him to keep up the momentum. Thus far he had not sustained more than six counts before the foot bag plopped to the concrete like an egg.

"No, idiot," Kenny said. "I realized that there are only one hundred days left of middle school. Then it's summer break and on to greener pastures."

Cash shifted in his seat but didn't say a word.

Brant gave up and tossed the Hacky Sack in the air.

"One hundred days sounds almost bearable," he said. He stopped. Looked at Cash. "I guess it's not a hundred days for you, though."

"Oh," Kenny said, realizing his m "Well, it's one hundred days of the schoo. for all of us."

"Yeah, but only *two* of us are moving on our lives." Brant tossed the Hacky Sack ag Up, down, up, down. "Seriously, Cash, what you gonna do if you fail again? I mean. Th would just be so messed up. You'll be old enough to drive, still in this craphole. Maybe they'd give you a parking space." He laughed. "What if you're as old as Mr. Stanecker by the time you get out?"

Mr. Stanecker was one of the school janitors. He looked like he was over two hundred years old.

"Ha. Ha. Very funny," said Cash.

"Sorry, bro. You know I'm just giving you a hard time," said Brant. "Seriously, though, I can't *wait* to get out of Park and check out the high school goods, if you know what I mean."

Kenny snorted. "You might check out the goods, but the goods won't check *you* out."

"Picture it," Brant continued. He stopped

tossing the Hacky Sack and put his hands up like a director framing a shot. "Girls. *New* girls. Hundreds of them coming from three different schools. Our options will be endless, Kenny." He shrugged at Cash. "Sorry, dude."

Kenny reached over and pushed Cash's shoulder good-naturedly. "There's something to be said for another year at Park." His smile widened mischievously. "For one thing, you'll be the older guy. Girls love that. They'll think you're, like, more mature. Older. Wiser."

"And dumber," Brant added.

Up, down, up, down.

Cash stood up. He'd had enough. Not that he'd ever let on. No, he'd keep acting casual. He could take it. This was how it always was with Brant and Kenny. They tortured one another over basketball, and they tortured one another over life. That was the way of things.

Sometimes the jokes didn't land very softly, though.

"I'm gonna take off," Cash said. Before anyone could protest, he added a quick lie. "I promised my dad I'd help him with something."

"With what?" Brant said. "Getting your brother committed?" He laughed.

"Not cool, Brant," said Kenny. He shook his head, his mouth a tight line.

"I heard he went straight-up cuckoo at school." Brant looked at Cash, the humor gone from his face. "Is it true they had to call the cops?"

"No," Cash said. "Get real."

Brant shrugged. "He's got a screw loose."

"So do you," said Kenny. "And we haven't had *you* committed."

Cash shoved his hands in his coat pockets and mumbled "not yet" as he turned for home.

HELLO, SHE'S HOME

When Bird walked through the door that evening, Cash and her father were in the living room, silently watching *Scarecrow and Mrs. King*, where characters Lee and Francine were protecting a spoiled tennis player whose father was being threatened by the Soviets. Cash and her father each had blank looks on their faces. Sometimes Bird wondered what would happen if she ever dismantled the television. Would she find one of those swinging pendulums inside, the kind hypnotists use to put people to sleep?

Bird opened her mouth to say *Hello, I'm home*, but decided not to bother. She unzipped her winter coat, slipped it on the peg by the front door, and walked down the hall toward her parents' room, where she knew she'd find her mother. Fitch's music thumped, muffled but blaring.

A basket of laundry sat on top of her parents'

bed. Her mother was folding clothes and separating them into piles. She hummed under her breath as she worked.

"Hey, Mom," Bird said. "I'm home."

Mrs. Thomas smiled. "Hey, there. Did you have a nice dinner?"

"Yep." Bird picked up one of her brother's shirts, folded it, and placed it gently on top of the appropriate pile. "We ate meat loaf."

"Nice."

"We all sat at the dinner table."

"Mm-hm."

Bird picked up another shirt. "We should try that sometime, don't you think? All eat dinner together?"

"Fold it horizontally first, Bird." Her mother took the shirt out of her hands and demonstrated. "Not vertically."

Bird reached for another one from the messy pile. "I could clear off the table. What do you think, Mom?"

Her mother had moved on to socks. She balled pairs together and pitched them into the basket.

"What do I think about what?"

Bird folded horizontally.

"Never mind," she said.

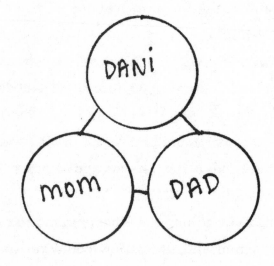

NEWS FOR BERNADETTE

Fitch spent the afternoon in his room, blasting U2 and reading a Choose Your Own Adventure, trying to push the previous day out of his mind, but inevitably he returned to Amanda. Her eyes, shiny with tears. The awkward way she ran out of the room. That's when he'd get a sick feeling in his gut, like he was on a roller coaster, but there was nothing fun or exciting about it. His brain added up all the reasons why everything was her fault (she refused to take a hint, she followed him to the arcade, she called him Henry and gave him stickers), but no matter what, he couldn't make the equation work. He didn't want to admit it, even to himself, but he had done something terrible, and that's all there was to it. On the way out of the principal's office, his mother had turned to him and said, "How could you be so cruel?" And that word—*cruel*—sliced him in half.

The sick feeling swirled and swirled and made him want to break things. His hands were full of nervous energy. If he could just break something, maybe it would go away.

He stretched out on his bed. Stared at the ceiling with his hands interlaced behind his head. He'd have to go back to school in two days. How would he face Amanda?

There was a knock on his bedroom door. He didn't say anything, hoping he'd imagined it. But there it was again.

"What," he said.

Bird came in, holding a stack of folded laundry. She closed the door with her foot then held up the clothes with one hand, like a waitress.

"I have some clothes for you," she said.

"Put them anywhere."

She set them down at the foot of his bed.

"So," she said. "What'd you do today?"

"Nothing."

He wanted to ask if people were talking about him at school, but then he'd have to admit that he cared.

"I went to Dani Logan's house. They let me stay for dinner."

"Fascinating."

"Her dad did a 'Cheers' for me. He said I could be the next Sally Ride."

"Who's Sally Ride?"

"The first woman in space."

Fitch didn't say anything.

"I told him I'd rather be Judith Resnik," Bird continued.

"Who's that supposed to be?"

Bird sighed, the same way Ms. Salonga did when he got an answer wrong.

"The mission specialist for *Challenger*. Remember?"

"No. Am I supposed to?"

"Ms. Salonga told us all about her. Plus, we talked about her the other night when we were looking at constellations. Remember, when I told you I was going to be the first—"

The nervous energy inside of Fitch sparked and itched.

"I got news for you, *Bernadette*. You're never gonna be a shuttle commander for NASA and you're never going into space. Reality check. You're just a girl from Delaware who's nothing special," said Fitch. He didn't know why he was saying it, but he couldn't stop the words from tumbling out, one by one, like poison. "You'll end up just like Mom. Not Sally Ride or Judith Whatever."

The words dangled in the air.

Fitch didn't move. Didn't make eye contact.

That sick feeling rose up again as Bird left the room.

Before she'd walked in, he'd wanted to break something.

And he had.

GIVE OR TAKE

Something about that number. The finality of it. One hundred. One hundred days until school was out. One hundred days until his friends went off to high school. One hundred days left of his seventh-grade encore.

It was hard to think about summer when it was frosty and wintry outside, but he thought about it anyway. How many days did summer have? The months yawned ahead of him. What long months those would be, with nothing to look forward to.

He heard Fitch's door open. Fitch talking to Bird. The door closing.

"Bird!" Cash called.

When she peeked her head inside his room, she had a strange look on her face. It was so different than her usual demeanor that Cash noticed for the first time that she *had* a demeanor.

"Are you okay?" he asked, which wasn't what he'd planned to say at all.

"I'm fine," she said. "Did you want something."

A sentence, not a question.

Cash had the distinct sense that his sister was *not* fine. Not at this moment, at least. But she would be. She always was.

"I was just wondering if you know how many days there are in summer vacation," he said.

Bird shifted her eyes to the floor as she calculated, then said, "About ninety-seven, I guess. Give or take."

He waited for her to ask why he wanted to know.

She didn't.

When she closed the door, Cash turned his attention to Dr. J.

"I wish all I had to do in life was get paid to play basketball," he said. "What's that like?"

But Dr. J didn't answer, of course.

SO BIG, SO SMALL

Bird: The universe has no beginning and no end. Just a vast space that goes on forever. A person could easily disappear into it. I think that's what is happening to me.

Judith Resnik: You're not disappearing. You're still here.

Bird: Isn't it strange?

Judith Resnik: Isn't what strange?

Bird: That a person can be surrounded by other people and still feel alone. You could be in a house full of people, even.

Judith Resnik: Loneliness is an emotion. It comes from inside, not outside.

Bird: Do you think Fitch is right? That I'm just a girl in Park, Delaware?

Judith Resnik: Well. You *are* a girl. You *do* live in Park, Delaware. I don't care for the word "just," though.

Bird: It's funny how small things can make a big difference.

Judith Resnik: You have many profound things to say, Bernadette Nelson Thomas. Has anyone ever told you that?

Bird: I don't think anyone's listening.

Judith Resnik: I am.

CASH MAKES A LIST

On the way to school, Cash stared out the front window while Bird sat quietly in the backseat. Mr. Thomas talked about Charles Barkley and how he would be the Sixers' star player when Dr. J retired. Before they left the house, his parents had argued nonstop for ten minutes about leaving Fitch home alone during his suspension. Mr. Thomas thought Mrs. Thomas should stay home with him. In response, Mrs. Thomas called him a "selfish, inconsiderate [expletive], because I have a job, too," and ultimately Fitch wound up at home by himself. Mrs. Thomas had scribbled out a note and left it on the kitchen island for him to find when he woke up.

It bewildered Cash how his dad could go from an angry tirade to a calm discussion about basketball in the space of a few minutes, but here he was, talking about Charles Barkley while Cash responded at all the right moments, agreeing here and nodding there. Normally he would be invested in the conversation, but his mental energy was currently focused on making lists.

He'd fallen asleep last night thinking about the one hundred days left of middle school and the long summer months, followed by another year at Park. Maybe if he had something going on in his life, like basketball or girls, the days wouldn't feel like endless hours of torture. That was his thought as he fell asleep. When he woke up, he realized something: the reason he didn't have anything going on was because he wasn't good at anything.

Ms. Salonga always told them that everyone was good at something. And he'd heard it before, from other teachers. He never thought much about it. But now, at this moment, it was all he could think about.

So far this was the only thing he could come up with:

Bird is good at school.

Fitch is good at arcade games.

I am good at nothing.

He would have settled for being good at *anything.* Anything at all.

He shifted his arm. It was itching again, and he had nothing to scratch it with.

When Mr. Thomas pulled up to the school, Bird and Cash said their obligatory good-byes and went their separate ways. Bird went wherever she went in the mornings. Cash went to the boys' bathroom. He washed his hands longer than usual so he could study his face in the mirror and psych himself up for the day ahead.

You will have something on your list by the end of the day, Cash Nelson Thomas.

Believe it.

THE WORLD IS HIS

Fitch wanted to be a housefly. He wanted to be so small that no one noticed him. He would fly into Ms. Salonga's class and sit on the walls and listen to what everyone said. Did they think he was a lunatic? What did Ms. Salonga say after he left? What did he care what Ms. Salonga thought, anyway?

When his mind veered toward Amanda and the words "fat, stupid cow," he reminded himself that he was home alone and the world was his.

He'd heard his parents' argument that morning, of course. He pulled the sheets over his head, still groggy from sleep, and listened. He hoped it would go in his favor, and it had. Everyone was gone. He was alone.

He found his mother's note in the kitchen. She would call around lunchtime, it said, and he better not even THINK (capital letters, underlined three times) about going to the arcade because she'd already talked to Mr. Hindley and he would call her if Fitch showed up. He grabbed the note with one hand, crumpled it, and left it sitting there, on the island, with all the other junk.

Now. What to do?

An empty house.

Just him. For hours.

First he stretched. He lifted his arms over his head and reached.

Then he drank two glasses of orange juice.

Then he walked into the living room.

He lifted a pillow from the sofa. He buried his head into it. And he screamed.

SOCIAL ORBIT

Bird was aware that there was a phenomenon called "going together," and that some of the girls had boyfriends, and some guys liked girls and vice versa and all that, but she never considered it part of her life. More like a cosmic event that happened outside of her solar system, which she would study with detached curiosity before going about her normal business. If people were "cute," she didn't notice. If "going together" was a social badge of honor, she didn't need it. It didn't occur to her to enter into this orbit herself. As far as she knew, it didn't occur to anyone else.

Until now.

"I think Devonte likes you," whispered Jessica Diaz toward the end of Ms. Salonga's class.

Bird wasn't too happy about the interruption, since Ms. Salonga was discussing the television broadcast of the *Challenger* launch.

"Some news stations are broadcasting the launch live, which is very exciting. And the principal has decided that a selected group of students—about a hundred or so—will be able to watch the launch live in the auditorium," Ms. Salonga was saying.

Jessica Diaz waved a hand in Bird's direction, as if to say, *hello, aren't you listening?*

Who could listen to Jessica Diaz during an announcement like this?

"You have to write an essay if you want to be considered," Ms. Salonga said.

Groans all around.

Some kids were already packing their books,

uninterested in the launch altogether, and certainly uninterested in writing an optional essay. But Bird was already mentally drafting hers—or she was trying to, anyway.

"Do you like him?" Jessica was saying.

"Who?" said Bird.

"*Devonte.* Duh."

Bird glanced at Devonte's desk, suddenly relieved that he was absent today. She wondered if he'd write an essay. The first sentence of hers came together. *One day, I will become NASA's first female shuttle commander.*

"I don't know," Bird said. "I never thought about it."

One day, I will become NASA's first female shuttle commander. The launch of the space shuttle Challenger *will be . . . will be . . .*

Will be what?

"Well." Jessica sighed. She had her books neatly stacked, ready to carry off to her next class. "You should."

She raised her eyebrows. For the first time, Bird noticed how much blue eyeshadow she wore. JB wore it, too. She saw it every time JB's eyes drifted closed. She occasionally nodded off during class. Sometimes Ms. Salonga called her on it. Sometimes not.

"If he likes you and you don't like him, you should save him the embarrassment and tell him sooner rather than later," Jessica said.

Bird's essay fell away, drifted off to another time, as she considered this new information.

"What if I *do* like him?" asked Bird.

"Then you'll have way bigger problems, don't you think?" Jessica said. "I mean . . . my dad would flip out if I entered into an *interracial* relationship." She said "interracial" very meticulously, like it was a new word that she'd just learned and she couldn't wait to use it in a sentence. "What would your parents do?"

Bird was about to reply when she realized she didn't know the answer.

NEVER-ENDING

The smoke alarm was the loudest thing Fitch had ever heard. It blared in his ears like a single, piercing wail, and it seemed never-ending. It took him by surprise when it started; he'd jumped back several feet and slammed his elbow into the counter. He cradled his elbow now and looked around frantically, trying to figure out how to make it stop.

All he'd wanted to do was fry an egg and make some toast. He'd shoved two slices of bread into the toaster and melted a lump of butter over the stove, just as he'd seen his mother do countless times. The eggs came out okay—a little burned and without the perfect yolk like he usually preferred, but edible enough as they sat dutifully on his plate—and he figured: Why not some bacon, too? But when he plopped the bacon onto the hot skillet, he didn't expect large plumes of smoke to sizzle into the air. And he certainly didn't expect the blaring alarm.

Could the entire neighborhood hear it?

He jumped from foot to foot, holding his elbow, his heart racing. He pulled a chair away from the dining room table. A stack of papers— who knew what—crashed from the seat to the floor, but there was no time to pick anything up. He steadied himself on the chair and fumbled with the alarm until the lid fell off, hitting him on the eyebrow. He cursed again and again until he finally fished the battery out and the alarm went quiet, all but the ringing in his ears. The house smelled like burned eggs and charred bacon. He wasn't even hungry anymore. He felt stupid for thinking he'd be able to cook. He should have just made himself a sandwich or something. He'd been so sure of himself. Big man home alone, cooking on the stove. He was embarrassed, even though there were no witnesses.

He could already hear the commentary and

remarks from his parents. *Did you use the stove?* his mother would ask, and she'd stomp over to investigate, sticking her nose near the burners to sniff. Then she'd list all the things that could have gone wrong. He could have burned down the house. Burned himself. Ruined the dishes. The list would be endless. *You're more trouble than you're worth sometimes,* she might say. She'd said that once.

He pivoted out of the kitchen. He would fix the alarm later. For now, he planned to go back into his room, his safe space, but his feet took him into his parents' bedroom instead. He stepped into their space, breathed deep. It smelled like his dad's aftershave. The bed wasn't made.

Fitch glanced toward the dresser, where his parents often kept loose change, and swiped three quarters and two dimes. He shoved the money deep into his pocket.

Now: to the closet.

Why did he go to their closet? He didn't know.

And why did he open the door and step inside? He didn't know. One motion followed the other, and he didn't think much about it.

He didn't turn on the light. He closed the door and nestled himself deep into the darkness. He was in a jungle of clothes. He sat down. He brought his knees to his chest and breathed. His mother's perfume. Laundry detergent. Shoes. His father. He pushed his back against the wall. Clothes dangled over his forehead. He used to stow away in here when he was little. The three of them—him, his sister, and brother—used to play hide-and-seek, and this was the first place he'd go. The hems didn't even reach the top of his head back then. It became known as his favorite hiding spot, but eventually, he got smart. Instead of throwing himself into the closet and closing the door with his heart pounding, he left the door open and stacked and arranged the clothes neatly around him—on his lap, all the way up to his chin and over his face—so he was completely camouflaged. Nothing to see here but a pile of dirty clothes, he'd think to himself.

But it never worked.

Bird always found him.

UNPRECEDENTED

Bird started with the unread magazines at the dining room table. *Life, Woman's Own, Time, Redbook.* She straightened the stacks, lifted them into her skinny arms, and carried them to the hallway closet, which was a chaotic mess of old sweaters, old shoes, old jackets, old everything, but had just enough room (if a few things were kicked to the side) for a few stacks of magazines.

She was on her second stack when Mrs. Thomas entered the kitchen with Cash at her heels. Burgers for dinner, and Cash did something completely unprecedented—he asked if he could help. Bird stopped midway through her stack straightening. She thought she misheard at first, but then he repeated himself.

"I've never cooked anything before," he said to their mother. "I wanna see if I'm any good at it."

Bird carried the next stack to the closet and set it down. Personally, she'd never had any interest in cooking. When she grew up, she planned to live on chips and sandwiches. She figured it would serve her well when she became an astronaut. You can't exactly have refined taste when you're floating in a space shuttle thousands of miles from Earth.

"What's triggered this sudden interest in home economics?" Mrs. Thomas said to Cash.

"I don't know. Just trying new things," he said.

Dishes clinked. The refrigerator door opened and closed as Bird gathered torn envelopes from mail that had been opened long ago.

"Who knows?" Cash continued. "Maybe I'm a great cook and don't even know it."

"Wash your hands first," Mrs. Thomas said. Pause. "Bird, what are you doing?—Cash, *really* wash your hands. Not fake wash. Bird—I asked you a question."

The faucet came on again.

"I'm clearing off the table," said Bird.

"Why?" Mrs. Thomas said.

Bird's hands slowly lost steam. She stopped gathering. Malfunction approaching.

"So we could eat dinner at the table," Bird replied.

Cash turned off the faucet. "Everyone at school is talking about what Fitch did," he said. "They say she started it."

"Make sure your hands are completely dry," Mrs. Thomas said. She was speaking to Cash, but still looking at Bird. "Stop doing that, Bird. I'll never be able to find anything."

"I heard she called *him* a name first," Cash continued. "He probably didn't even deserve to get suspended."

"He deserved it," said Mrs. Thomas.

When she turned around to keep making dinner, Bird sat down and stared at the table. One corner was clear. What a grand success. She thought about how she'd launched herself into space in Ms. Salonga's class.

Copy. Copy.

She thought about what Jessica Diaz said about Devonte.

"Can I have bacon on mine?" Cash asked.

"You don't need bacon," Mrs. Thomas said.

Bird decided to launch herself out of her current environment and into the living room, where her father was silently watching *The A-Team.* They stared at the screen together. Captain Murdock was feared kidnapped, which was unfortunate because he was desperately needed to steal a Russian helicopter.

Sounds from the kitchen drifted into orbit.

"There's no bacon," Cash said.

"I just bought some."

"Dad must have eaten it."

"No, he didn't."

"Well, there's none in here."

"You aren't looking hard enough."

Cash was now at the skillet while their mother looked for bacon.

"Dad," said Bird. She cleared her throat. "Can I ask you a hypothetical question?"

The question was on Bird's tongue: Is it okay to like someone who is different from you? Ever since she'd had that conversation with the girls at school, she realized she didn't know. Even if she didn't like Devonte, the question felt important.

He didn't respond. He was too entranced by the invisible pendulum inside the TV.

She was about to repeat herself, but Mrs. Thomas's voice filled the room instead.

"Mike, did you eat the bacon?"

Bird held her breath. Sometimes, all it took was a single question to turn Dr. Jekyll into Mr. Hyde.

Mr. Thomas grumbled and called back, "What?"

"Did you eat the bacon?"

"No!"

"I just bought some, and now it's gone!"

Bird's eyes drifted from her mother to her father as they hollered questions and answers at each other. The shift of the house could be imperceptible, but Bird was an astute observer. Thoughts of Devonte fell away.

"I'll alert the media," Mr. Thomas mumbled.

From the kitchen: "What did you say?"

Bird darted out of the living room and to the kitchen island, where she sat down on a stool.

"He said he didn't eat any bacon, Mom," she said, quickly adding, "The burgers smell good, Cash."

To be honest, they smelled charred. Cash

pressed on the meat, despite being told not to. Mrs. Thomas slammed the fridge door and hurried to the stove. She shooed him away.

"I *told you* not to press down on the patties like that," she said. "It burns them." She shook her head.

"I thought it would cook it faster." He shrugged. "We'll give the burned one to Fitch." He nodded toward the hallway, where their brother's door was closed, and smiled conspiratorially at Bird.

Mrs. Thomas lifted each of the patties with the spatula.

"If we clear off the table, we can all eat together," Bird said.

Mrs. Thomas straightened her back and released a single, exasperated sigh.

"These are all burned," she said. "You're not exactly the world's best chef."

Bird smiled at her brother. "Not yet, anyway," she said.

But Cash's smile had wandered away.

LEGENDARY

The air was charged when Fitch walked in. He expected as much. He'd planned for it. It went just as he suspected. All eyes were on him. They followed him from door to desk. The stares burned as he passed by. He'd purposely arrived just before the tardy bell, had even avoided Vern before class, so he wouldn't make a fuss. But there was a fuss anyway.

Not just stares. Whispers, too. He heard them the moment he got to school. Girls nudging each other. Giggles. Fingers pointing, even. His cheeks warmed with embarrassment. He didn't want the attention. He wanted to erase everything. He wanted to push it far away until it disappeared into the galaxy and evaporated into a black hole. But he couldn't, and he couldn't stop thinking about Amanda.

What would he say when he saw her?

What would he do?

What would *she* say? What would *she* do?

He sat down and pretended like her desk wasn't there inches away from his, even though it gaped at him, waiting for her arrival.

"Dude, everyone is flipping out over what happened," Vern said. He, too, shifted his eyes to Amanda's desk. "People are saying the cops took you away in handcuffs." He grinned. "You're a legend."

Fitch couldn't read Vern's expression. It was somewhere between awe and jealousy. He wanted to see something negative there, something that judged him and matched what he felt inside, but there was no negativity on Vern's face.

In fact, most of the looks thrown his way were full of questions, not judgment.

What, exactly, was legendary about what he'd done?

"Amanda switched classes," said Vern.

Fitch kept his expression blank, but his heart thundered. "What do you mean?"

"Ms. Salonga gave her a choice. Either you could switch classes, or she could."

Fitch wanted to be that housefly again. He wanted to land on the wall and listen to Ms. Salonga's conversation with Amanda.

"She should've made *me* switch," Fitch said. "I'm the one who . . . "

He let the sentence float.

When Rachel Hill came into the room, he didn't even notice her smile at him.

KID ON THE MOVE

Mr. Wills, the famously monotonous social studies teacher, gave Cash a hall pass with little fanfare. When Cash wandered into the hall, he felt a strange jolt of adrenaline. He didn't need the hall pass, of course. But anything was better than being in class, where teachers asked questions he never knew the answers to, and he spent most of the time feeling like an idiot. Out here, in the hall, he wasn't stupid. He was just Cash Nelson Thomas, kid on the move.

After going into the boys' bathroom, where he washed his hands and stared at himself in the mirror for longer than he'd ever admit, he made his way to the trophy case. He wanted to look at the basketball trophy again. He didn't understand why he tortured himself this way, but there it was.

The trophy was on the second shelf, as always, standing tall with the others. A shiny reminder that the team didn't need him to win.

You can run, but you can't shoot. And if you can't shoot . . .

Well. If you can't shoot, what's the point of playing basketball? That was the long and short of it.

He was still staring at that stupid trophy when a voice shot over his head, making him jump.

"How goes it, Thomas?"

Cash knew who it was before he even turned around, and sure enough, there was Coach, standing there smiling.

"Hey, Coach," said Cash, all casual. He tried to shove both hands in his pockets, before he remembered that the cast wouldn't allow his right hand to be shoved anywhere. He shifted from foot to foot instead. How embarrassing to be discovered here, at this moment, by the very person who knew his failures all too well.

Coach nodded toward the cast. "How's the arm?"

"Not bad. Getting used to it." That was the truth,

too. Penny L/S Charlie didn't grate at him like it had last week, even though the letters were still big and bold and in his direct line of vision at all times.

"We miss you on the team this year." Coach smiled.

Cash knew that was a lie, and he knew the smile was fake, but he also knew that people lied sometimes to make other people feel better.

Coach was a nice guy, but the smile and the lie only made Cash feel worse.

When Cash didn't respond, Coach kept talking. "The year goes by fast, huh? Seems like it was just football season. Soon it'll be track. Then it all starts up again." He shook his head. "Each year moves faster than the next."

God, Cash hoped that was true. He wanted next year to move faster than the speed of light.

"Yeah," Cash said, since he felt like he was supposed to say something.

"Well," said Coach. "You better get to class soon, yeah?"

Cash nodded. Smiled. He watched Coach walk down the hall but continued to stand there for the next few minutes. He wasn't ready to go back to Mr. Wills. He didn't want to slip back into the classroom shackles.

Not yet.

BAD BOY

Fitch could destroy robots and enemy ships. He could grab extra oxygen on his way to the nuclear reactor and get out before it exploded. But the maze was his enemy. The maze was his kryptonite. You had to fly the ship through it without getting zapped or shot. The twists and turns seemed to come out of nowhere. No matter how prepared he felt, they emerged to annihilate him.

He wasn't doing his best, anyway. His eyes were focused on Major Havoc, but his brain floated somewhere else. He hadn't seen Amanda all day, and he certainly didn't expect to see her here, but he looked around anyway. When he passed Skee-Ball, he looked. When he grabbed a quick bag of popcorn, he looked. Every time a crop of brown hair moved in his peripheral vision, he looked. He didn't know why he was looking for her, or what he would do if he saw her. He tried to imagine himself apologizing, but the image wouldn't formulate. He tried to imagine saying "hey, Amanda" as if nothing had happened, but that didn't seem right, either. So what did he expect to accomplish?

It took him forty-five minutes to spend all his quarters. When he had, he wiped his hands down the front of his jeans and decided to walk around. Vern hadn't come today and there wasn't much else to do, but he didn't want to go home.

He wandered by Galaga, Pole Position, Centipede, and Pac-Man.

He wandered by the popcorn machine again.

When he made his way to pinball row, Mr. Hindley smiled widely at him. He was standing next to Bright Star One with the crumpled "OUT OF ORDER" sign in his hand. The bulbs flashed: READY FOR TAKEOFF.

"Patron Thomas," Mr. Hindley said. He patted the top of the machine. "Our friend is back. How about a game? Give her a test run?"

"I'm out of quarters," said Fitch. "Maybe next time."

"Eh, I'm sure you wouldn't want to try her out again anyway. To be honest, I don't know why I bothered with this thing," said Hindley. "No one plays them."

Fitch eyed the line of machines. Five in all.

"Have you ever thought of selling them?" Fitch asked. "You could use the money to buy more games, like Alpha Mission or Battle City. You could even get a stand-up pinball game."

"That wouldn't make any sense," Mr. Hindley

said. "Why would I get a pinball cabinet when I have actual pinball right here?"

Fitch shrugged. "Just a thought."

"Mark my words, Fitch—one day, someone is gonna march in here and become the next pinball wizard. Next thing you know, it's—"

Mr. Hindley's words drifted away as he eyed something over Fitch's shoulder. His face morphed into a knowing smile.

"We'll talk more later," he said, patting Fitch's shoulder.

Suddenly Fitch was sandwiched by the Jessicas.

"Oh," he said.

The girls each held a Coke with gloss-stained straws.

Jessica Diaz flashed a toothy smile. "Hey, Fitch."

"Uh," mumbled Fitch.

JB took a sip of her drink. "Welcome back."

"Welcome back where?" Fitch said, his throat dry.

"To school, silly," JB replied. "After your . . . *suspension.*"

The way she whispered it and grinned made him uncomfortable. He cleared his throat.

"We heard what happened," JB continued. "We know she started the whole thing. It's so unfair that you were suspended for two days."

"Uh," Fitch said.

He felt like Major Havoc, trapped in a maze, not sure what he was supposed to do or say next.

"Anyway," Jessica Diaz said. She glanced at her friend then at Fitch. "We were wondering something."

Fitch asked what. At least he thought he did. He couldn't quite tell if his mouth was moving. Did he look as nervous as he felt?

JB bit her straw. She lifted it up with her teeth then released it. "Do you . . . like anyone?"

Fitch's hands were sweating. "Like anyone?"

"Yeah. You know. *Like.*"

"Oh." He wished Mr. Hindley would come back. It was much more comfortable talking to him than the Jessicas. He felt warm and exposed, like a giant spotlight was shining over him. "No."

The Jessicas' faces brightened. Apparently, he'd answered correctly.

"Good," Jessica Diaz said. "Because someone likes you, and we were wondering if you'd be interested in her."

JB rolled her eyes. "Of course he will be." She fiddled with her straw again. "Do you want to know who it is?"

Fitch had no response. He was still trying to process the words coming out of their mouths.

"Okay," he said, finally.

"It's Rachel," JB said. She bounced on her toes as if this were the most exciting news of the century. Maybe it was. *"Rachel Hill."*

Fitch stared at her blankly.

Was this some kind of joke?

"Uh." Fitch shoved his hands in his pockets.

"She told me today," JB continued. "Apparently she has a thing for *bad boys,* as she put it."

"Bad boys," Fitch repeated. The words landed on his ears, but made no logical sense. Rachel Hill. Him. Bad boys. Fitch started a sentence. "I'm not . . ."

When he didn't continue, the girls simply stared at him. Their bright expressions dissolved into confusion. Jessica Diaz cocked her head to one side like a dog who had just heard an unfamiliar noise.

"It's Rachel Hill," she said. "Don't you like her?"

Like her? He'd never even spoken to her. He'd never even *considered* speaking to her. Rachel was in a different galaxy.

What did it mean to like someone, anyway?

He thought of Vern, with his buttered fingers and starry-eyed crush.

"Uh," said Fitch. "I'm not really looking for a girlfriend."

The Jessicas' mouths dropped open in unison. He'd never seen two people look more startled. It was as if he'd set fire to a million dollars. They looked like they were about to say something else, but Fitch's attention had shifted to a tall girl with brown hair who was standing near Asteroids. She turned around.

It wasn't Amanda.

He exhaled.

"I gotta go," he said.

He stepped around the Jessicas, heart pounding, and left them standing in the blinking lights of Bright Star One.

A FINE LINE

There was a line on Cash's bedroom wall. He couldn't remember when he'd put it there. Last year, maybe. It was a faint, simple hash mark, pretty high up, drawn with pencil. It served as a goal line of sorts. Something for him to aspire to. The day his fingertips grazed this line, he reasoned, was the day he would be a worthwhile basketball player. Someone to make Dr. J proud as he watched from his poster on the opposite side of the room. The distance between Cash's fingertips and that hash mark may as well have been a mile, though. He never even got close.

For a while the hash mark taunted him. A visual reminder of his athletic failures. But he never erased it. Eventually he learned to ignore it.

He couldn't remember the last time he faced it the way he did now.

Surely he'd improved.

Surely he'd grown.

Surely he could do it now.

He bounced up and down and loosened his shoulders. He wiggled the tips of his fingers on his right hand, which jutted out of his cast like stunted sausages.

This time he would hit his mark, even if he reinjured his wrist in the process.

He took a deep breath and went for it.

He wasn't even close.

He could almost hear Dr. J sigh.

When he turned around, swearing under his breath, Bird was in the doorway.

"Mom is picking up KFC for dinner," she said. "What're you doing?"

Cash would have been embarrassed if it was anyone but Bird.

"Nothing," he said. "Just working on my jump shot, I guess. Not that it matters."

He sat down with his back against the wall. He kept talking, though he didn't know why.

"I'm not good at anything," he continued. Yes, he knew he was feeling sorry for himself, but he didn't care. He counted off on his fingers. "I suck at school. I can't shoot. I can't jump. I can't even cook a freakin' hamburger." His neck burned. "The only thing I can do is run." *Run away from homework. Run away from points.*

Bird shrugged. "Well, there you go."

"What do you mean, there I go?"

"You just said you were good at running."

Cash snorted. "Yeah. Running from homework. Running from passing grades. Sure. Lots of good that does, Bird. Thanks for the pep talk." He leaned his head against the wall.

"Maybe you're just playing the wrong game," she said.

And then she closed the door.

THE FINAL FRONTIER

Bird's essay got her a seat in the auditorium. Devonte and Dani got seats, too. The launch was only three days away now—Thursday, to be exact. Ms. Salonga reminded them by tapping the chalkboard, where she had the date underlined.

"We've been talking a lot about space travel this month, but we haven't answered one very important question," Ms. Salonga said, leaning against the corner of her desk. "It's a question that's foremost on many Americans' minds. And it's a very simple question: Why? Why are we going into space? Why are we spending so much money to send astronauts there?"

A few kids shot their hands into the air, but Ms. Salonga waved them away and said that they all needed to join their space crews to brainstorm answers to these questions. Each crew was expected to come up with at least five valid and well-considered reasons why space exploration was important. The shuttle commander would be in charge of writing down the answers and coaxing participation from all crew members.

Chairs scraped against the floor as everyone moved into their circles. When Devonte scooted his desk closer to hers, Bird's heart pounded. *Tha-thump. Tha-thump.* The prospect of watching the launch was the only thing that prevented Bird from having a full-on anxious spiral every time she was around Devonte. She tried to focus on something else. She kept her eyes on Christopher and Marcus as they joined the circle. Christopher was wearing Aerosmith today.

Once everyone was settled, Dani opened her notebook.

"Who wants to go first?" she said.

They all looked at Bird, but her brain wasn't in the game. She was too aware of Devonte's presence.

"I got one," Devonte said. "Space exploration is important because we might run out of room."

Dani wrote this down but looked skeptical. "What do you mean?"

"On Earth," Devonte said. "If it gets too crowded, we'll run out of room. And then where will we go?"

Jessica Diaz rolled her eyes. Bird couldn't be sure, but it seemed like she rolled them at her, not at him, as if she, Bird, was somehow responsible for anything Devonte said.

"Duh, Devonte. It would take *forever* for us to 'run out of room.' There are, like, a million places humans can go."

Devonte crossed his arms. "Name one."

"Think about all the places in the world where no one lives. Like, mountains or rain forests or something."

JB nodded.

Christopher said, "Yeah, there's room *now*. But what happens when there's four times as many people?"

"Exactly," Devonte replied.

Dani erased what she'd originally written and said, "I'm going to put 'in case of overpopulation.'"

Devonte grinned at the Jessicas in triumph.

"What else?" Dani said.

"Life on other planets," JB said. "Like, we need to go into space to see if there's anybody out there."

"What difference does it make if there's life out there or not?" Christopher asked. "We've got life-forms right here on Earth that don't make any sense."

Marcus and Devonte laughed.

"It's *important* that we know if there are aliens

in the universe," JB said. "What if we want to be friends with them?"

"E.T.'s spaceship went exploring, and those white-coat dudes almost killed him," Christopher said.

"Whatever," Jessica said. "He became *friends* with Elliott, which was the whole point of the movie anyway."

Dani wrote "befriend aliens" in her notebook.

Bird cleared her throat. "Resources," she said.

She couldn't remember ever feeling nervous around her classmates the way she did right now. All because of Devonte and his crush. She decided then and there, as Dani wrote 'resources,' that no good could come from liking someone that way.

"What do you mean by 'resources'?" Jessica Diaz asked.

"Well," Bird began. "There's a chance we could run out of resources at some point. Because of overpopulation, or whatever." Devonte smiled at this acknowledgment, but she ignored him. "In hundreds of years or something, we might not have any more resources on Earth. If we find planets that have resources, like fuel and water and stuff, we'd have a backup plan."

They all nodded.

"I've got another one," said Christopher, pointing to Dani's notebook. "If we don't go into space, other countries will. What if the Russians go out there and find an entire planet made out of killer nuclear gas? They'd get to it before us. We should be number one."

Dani wrote down "world domination." Everyone nodded in agreement.

"That's four," said Dani. "We need at least one more."

No one offered anything. Not even Bird. Her mind was still preoccupied.

After several seconds of silence, Dani's eyes landed on Marcus Sturgess, who'd been silently doodling in his notebook.

"What about you, Marcus?" she said, her voice uncertain. "Can you think of anything?"

He shrugged.

"We just need one more," said Dani.

A new electricity filled the air. Marcus flew so far under the radar, people often forgot he was there. And he often wasn't. But today, here he was, sitting in his seat, under the scrutinizing eyes of his fictional space mates. He glanced up, but only for a moment.

"It's stupid," he finally mumbled.

Dani raised her eyebrows. "What's stupid?"

"Space exploration," he said. "Ms. Salonga wants us to come up with reasons why it makes sense for us to go into space, but it *doesn't* make sense."

If Marcus were a machine, Bird thought, he'd be something that made the air heavy. Like a humidifier.

"There are big things in space," Marcus continued. "Asteroids. Meteorites. Comets. Think about how huge the universe is. Ms. Salonga said it was more than ninety-billion light years in diameter. Then think about how small we are. We're practically nothing. A giant fireball could be out there, headed directly for us, and we wouldn't be able to do anything about it. Not a single thing."

The Jessicas simultaneously turned toward the classroom window, as if Marcus had just summoned a fireball outside.

"Oh," Dani said.

Bird sank a little in her seat. She felt like she was shrinking right then and there, shrinking and shrinking, smaller and smaller, while the universe around them swelled and swelled.

We're practically nothing.

"We still need one more," JB said. Her voice sounded distant.

Did she feel it, too?

Dani cleared her throat. "In *Star Trek*, they call space the 'final frontier,'" she said.

"We've explored all over Earth. Space is the last big mystery." Pause. "Do you think that's a reason?"

Everyone nodded. All but Marcus.

Bird watched intently as Dani wrote "final frontier" in her notebook.

HEY, COACH

Cash typically moved quickly to get a good spot in the lunch line, but today he breezed past the cafeteria on his way to the gym. Coach Farnsworth's office was just outside the basketball court, where Cash had once run laps around Kenny and Brant. The door was open. His desk was covered with binders, lanyards, and a half-eaten sandwich. He sat behind it with

Time open in front of him. "Skywatch: Halley's Comet Swings By," the cover read.

"Hey, Coach," said Cash.

Coach looked up and smiled. One side of his face was round with food. He chewed and said, "Hey there, Thomas. What can I do for you?"

Cash glanced toward the basketball court, then stepped inside. He hadn't been in Coach's office since the day he was dropped from the team. *We'd love to keep you,* Coach had said, *but if you don't maintain a two-point-oh grade-point average, you can't play sports. That's the rules.* The words had filled the room. At the time Cash had wondered if Coach was secretly thrilled that his GPA had dropped. It was an easy way to get him off the court. It didn't seem like Coach's style—he was a good guy, always propping them up, encouraging them to do their best—but you never know what's going on inside a person's head and heart.

"Um." Cash shifted from foot to foot. "I was

thinking about something and wanted to get your thoughts on it."

Coach closed the magazine, leaned back in his chair, and opened his arms wide as he swallowed the rest of his bite. "Shoot."

"Well . . ." Cash took a breath. "I was thinking about what you said when I was on the team, about me being a good runner and all . . ."

"Yep. If I remember correctly, you had a six-minute mile."

". . . and I was just thinking . . . I mean, well, I was wondering, or considering . . ." He hadn't meant to sound so unsure, but his next words left his mouth as a question. ". . . the track team?"

Coach leaned forward and raised his eyebrows.

Uh-oh, Cash thought. *This is the part where I get laughed out of the office. Give it up, Thomas, he'll say. You're not an athlete. How many more ways can I break it to you?*

"You've always been hung up on basketball," said Coach.

"Yeah, well. I was thinking of changing the game, I guess."

Coach smiled. A big, genuine smile.

"Good thinking," he said. "Track just might be your thing. Tryouts aren't till March, so you've got a while to prepare. Best part is . . ." He motioned toward Cash's arm. "That cast won't stop you from training."

Cash smiled, too.

"Just one thing, Thomas," Coach said. He pointed to Cash's backpack. "Your grades. You know the rules, right?"

"Yes, Coach. Two-point-oh grade-point average to play any sports."

Coach nodded. "Doesn't matter what sport it is. Rule's the same for track as it is for basketball. But that won't be a problem." He cocked his head to the side. "Right, Thomas?"

Now it was Cash's turn to nod. "Right, Coach."

I TOUCH THE FUTURE

Bird: I finished another schematic today. My Dad's old Walkman. But I couldn't focus. I have so many thoughts in my mind at once.

Judith Resnik: Like what?

Bird: Well. Today I mostly kept thinking about what Marcus said, about how big the universe is and how small we are.

Judith Resnik: The universe is big. Humans are small. We knew that already.

Bird: I know, but . . . he said other stuff, too. Afterward I just keep thinking and thinking about it. I guess it bothers me that we're just specks of dust floating in an enormous void.

Judith Resnik: That's one way of putting it.

Bird: There has to be a reason for it all, right? I mean. You're not just going into space for *nothing* or just for *fun* or so we can dominate the world or something.

Judith Resnik: Of course not.

Bird: What would *you* have said to Marcus? What should I have said?

Judith Resnik: I would have told him that quote from Christa McAuliffe. You know the one I'm talking about. Ms. Salonga has it written on a Post-it note, stuck to her desk.

Bird: Yes. I know it.

Judith Resnik: Christa said, "I touch the future." That's what we're doing, Bernadette.

Touching the future.

Bird: I like that.

Judith Resnik: Me, too.

Bird: Good night, Judith.

Judith Resnik: Good night, Bird.

Thursday, January 23, 1986

COLLECT YOUR THOUGHTS

The *Challenger* launch had been rescheduled, but that didn't stop Ms. Salonga from droning on about it for the entire week. By the time Thursday came around, the weekend was on the horizon and Fitch decided to sink all his lunch money—and a few quarters he swiped from his parents' dresser—into Major Havoc after school, with the singular goal of beating his high score. The time for distractions was over. He hadn't caught a single glimpse of Amanda. That had to be a sign for him to forget what had happened and move on. It's not like he'd *murdered* someone, after all.

Once he'd decided on a plan, the school day seemed endless, and it had only just begun. Ms. Salonga stood at the front of the room, talking about astrograms, which sounded like something from *The Jetsons*.

"How many of you believe in life on other planets?" she asked, tossing her chalk from one hand to the other. He knew she had applied for the Teacher in Space program, and he tried to imagine what it'd be like to see her in an astronaut suit, shooting off into the stars. It was a strange picture.

Most people raised their hands. Fitch didn't. Not because he didn't believe in life on other planets, but because he didn't much care either way. Maybe he'd start worrying about life on other planets when he figured out life on Earth.

"It would be incredible if we could find out whether or not you're right," Ms. Salonga continued. "Some astronomers believe that there could be as many as ten million habitable places in our galaxy. But they also say there could be as few as twenty. And, of course, it's possible that there's only one—Earth. We don't have the technology yet to travel to distant planets in search of life. But we *do* have the technology to communicate with them. Or try to, at least. One example is the radio telescope at the Arecibo Observatory in Puerto Rico. It sent its first message into space in nineteen seventy-four in an attempt to find extraterrestrial life. We call these messages 'astrograms.'"

Rachel's hand shot up. "What do the astrograms say?" she asked.

Ms. Salonga answered—something about our solar system, and sketches of technology—but Fitch's mind wandered as he gazed at Rachel's ponytail from his seat at the back of the room. Her interest in him had been fleeting. He hadn't heard another word about the whole thing from either of the Jessicas. Certainly not from Rachel. But that didn't mean she wasn't a topic of conversation. Vern's flame burned brighter with each passing day.

"I called her again last night," he'd told Fitch just that morning. "She said she couldn't talk because she had homework, but she asked for my number to call me back."

"Did she call you back?" Fitch asked.

Vern's smile drifted away. "No, but I bet she does tonight."

Fitch had told him not to count on it. He hadn't meant it to sound sharp, though it came out that way.

"You're just jealous because the only girls you can get are the ones who look like Big Bird," Vern said.

At that moment, Fitch had wanted to push Vern. Hard. Partly because Vern was cutting on him and partly because he was cutting on Amanda. It didn't make sense, and he knew that.

Fitch had cut on Amanda worse than anyone—so much so that she'd apparently dropped off the face of the Earth—so what right did he have to defend her now?

It occurred to Fitch that he could shut Vern up by telling him that—as of one week ago—Rachel liked him, Fitch, but he kept it to himself.

Ms. Salonga took a stack of index cards from her desk and held them up, which was a surefire sign that they were all about to be forced to participate in some sort of activity. He hoped and prayed that it wasn't another crew assignment. He'd trade every quarter in his pocket to get out of another one of those.

Luckily, he didn't have to.

This was to be a solo project.

"I want you to take this index card and write your own astrogram," Ms. Salonga said as she walked around the room, passing them out. "Think about what you want to say. *Really* think. What do you want to share about life on this planet? What would you want other life-forms to know? What is most important for them to understand if they're going to survive in our environment? There are limits to what you can say, just as there are limits for scientists. You only have the room on this card. One side only. What will you share with the rest of the galaxy?"

Some kids were writing before she'd even finished talking.

"Take your time," she reminded everyone. "Collect your thoughts."

Fitch stared at the blank card.

He collected his thoughts.

He picked up his pencil.

WHAT PLANET ARE WE ON?

Except for holidays, the Nelson Thomas family had never—not once—sat down for dinner together. Yes, Bird had cleared the junk off the table—a corner of it, at least—but that didn't encourage anyone to break bread around it. Her efforts hadn't been wasted, though. Cash now sat at the table with *Earth Science* open in front of him. He had a pencil awkwardly grasped in his right hand as he attempted to maneuver a notebook with his cast, a skill he had yet to master.

When Mrs. Thomas came home from work, she set her purse on the kitchen island as usual. She eyed her eldest son suspiciously.

He looked up. "Hey, Mom, did you know that Venus is the third-brightest object in the sky, after the sun and moon?"

She glanced back at the front door, as if she'd accidentally stepped through a portal to another universe.

"What planet am I on?" she said.

ASTROGRAM

The air is made of oxygen, but don't worry because it isn't toxic. We have gravity so you might feel heavier at first. Or lighter, depending on your home planet. Humans come in all kinds so we might look different from each other but we are really the same. You can eat plants and some of the animals, but not humans. We want to be your friends so don't be scared. You are safe here.   Sincerely, Bird Thomas

Astrogram   Fitch 2.

                    Go back.
                    Trust me.

MOMENT OF TRUTH

It was the moment of truth.

When Ms. Salonga's class ended, Bird tapped Devonte on the shoulder as he gathered up his books and asked if she could talk to him for a second. He looked momentarily confused.

"Sure, Bird," he said.

She saw the Jessicas and Dani in her peripheral vision but chose not to acknowledge them. She could practically *feel* Dani's curiosity. They hadn't discussed Devonte in any real way; for whatever reason, Bird wasn't interested in making boys the center of any conversation. She'd rather listen to Dani talk about *Star Trek* for two hours straight.

One day—maybe—Bird would want to travel in the social orbit of boyfriendhood.

But not today.

The crowd in the classroom thinned. Bird and Devonte had some privacy as they walked toward the hall side by side. Bird walked slowly. Devonte followed her lead.

She didn't say anything for several steps.

"So . . . " Devonte finally said. "What did you wanna talk about?"

Bird hugged her books to her chest. They'd reached the classroom door. She motioned him over to the wall so they wouldn't get gobbled by the hallway traffic. Now it was Ms. Salonga in her peripheral vision, only she wasn't there long—she went into the hallway to greet her next class.

"I have something to tell you," Bird said. She

looked at her feet, then at Devonte. She cleared her throat. "I don't *like*-like you. But I really like being your friend."

Devonte raised his eyebrows. For a moment, his face froze. His eyeballs were the first thing to move. He looked right, then left. Like he was searching the air for words.

Bird's heart banged harder than ever. She sensed something terrible on the horizon. A little voice that whispered: *something incredibly embarrassing is about to happen to you.*

And she was right.

"Uh . . . okay," said Devonte. His face relaxed. It turned into something else. Bemusement. "But . . . I don't like you, either, Bird. I mean. Not in that way."

"Oh," Bird said. "Oh."

"You're nice and everything. You're just not really the kind of girl that I'd, you know, *like*."

Noise from the hall drifted toward them— laughter and a whistle.

"Oh," Bird said.

What did he mean?

She wanted to ask, but didn't know how to form the words, and why did she care anyway? Wasn't this what she wanted—to not be someone's girlfriend?

"You're just, kinda, *plain*. You know?" Devonte said. His expression instantly morphed into one of regret. "I don't mean that in a bad way. I just . . ." He sighed. "You're not . . ." He shrugged. "Anyway. I guess what I'm saying is—yes, we can be friends."

"Oh," Bird said. That one syllable was the only sound she was capable of making, apparently.

"See you around," he said. He turned on his heel.

She watched him walk away.

THE GOD OF HAVOC

Marsh pushed his glasses up his nose and said, "You're a god."

Fitch had just finished his best run on Major Havoc yet. Vern and Marsh were at his side.

"No joke, that was awesome," said Vern.

Fitch almost smiled. He was proud, to be sure, but lately every moment of his day had been colored by a vague sense of disappointment. Disappointment in what? He wasn't sure. But for the past month, maybe longer, a fog had descended.

"When are you gonna teach me how to play?" asked Marsh.

The kid had called him a god. Half joking, sure, but the way Marsh looked up at him, blinking behind those thick, ridiculous glasses, made him feel like anything but.

Fitch gestured toward Pop-A-Shot. "You can't even make *one* basket, and you think you can play *this*?" He shook his head. "Get serious, Marsha."

Vern laughed.

Marsh's look of admiration turned into something else. Well, good. Anything was better than that stupid little-brother look.

"Yeah," Marsh said. He threw a quick wave over his shoulder before making his way to Ms. Pac-Man.

YOU'RE NOT

Bird had been looking for something to dismantle when she found the old music box on the top shelf of her closet. It had been a gift for her ninth birthday.

"See?" her mother had said, with the box carefully balanced on her lap. "You turn the crank and it plays a song. If you're ever upset, you can escape right into the notes."

A week later, when one of her parents' arguments swelled and swelled until their words bounced off every wall in the house, Bird turned the crank until her fingers were sore. But it wasn't enough to drown out the sound of her parents. Eventually she'd stowed the music box away in her closet. Now it was in pieces on her desk, next to a half-finished schematic. She wanted to finish. She wanted to make sense of all the parts. But she couldn't stop replaying the morning over and over in her mind.

You're just . . . plain.

That was bad enough, but the words that followed were much worse. They orbited her now as she sat at her desk, unmoving. Fitch's muffled music seeped through the wall.

You're not . . .

Those were quite possibly the two most terrible words to start any sentence.

You're not pretty.

You're not interesting.

You're not special.

The possible endings were as vast as the night sky.

Fitch's music stopped.

The silence felt heavy, as if it was coming from deep within Bird herself.

You're just . . . a girl from Delaware.

Being pretty isn't your thing.

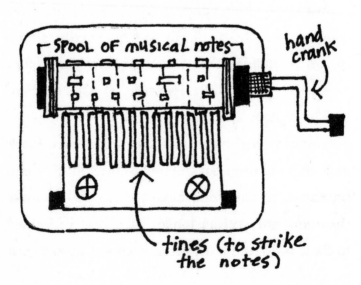

BIRD'S-EYE VIEW:
MUSIC BOX

SPOOL OF MUSICAL NOTES

hand crank

tines (to strike the notes)

A SHORT LIST OF PIPERS

Next door, hidden away in his own room, Fitch inhaled the scent of the Park, Delaware, phone book, and blared AC/DC as loud as he could.

The phone book smelled like newspaper. His index finger and thumb were smeared with ink from turning the pages. The short list of Pipers glared at him accusingly.

Amanda wasn't individually listed, which wasn't a surprise, but there were eight Pipers total, each with a different number. One of them had to be Amanda's family, right?

An old tabletop phone sat between Fitch and his boom box. The phone had been banished to the linen closet last year because the mouthpiece was loose. Bird had promised to fix it (and she had, after taking it apart), but by then they had a new phone and this one was forgotten. Fitch had snatched it out of the closet right after swiping the phone book from the kitchen.

He plugged the phone in now, quietly and slowly, and picked up the receiver. The dial tone came through loud and clear. Ominous, almost.

He replaced the cradle, cracked his knuckles, and studied the list of Pipers. *Piper, Adam. Piper, Coretta. Piper, Harold & Margaret. Piper, Oden. Piper, Richard. Piper, Rose.*

He reached over to the boom box and turned off the music. *Click.*

Silence.

He cleared his throat. Swallowed away a dry patch. Ran his sweaty hands over his jeans.

Picked up the phone. *Piper, Adam.*

It rang three times before a man picked up. Adam Piper, presumably.

"Hello?" Presumably Adam Piper said.

At first Fitch thought he wouldn't be able to speak. Then he blurted out: "Is Amanda there?"

The man paused. "Amanda who?"

Fitch hung up.

Shook out his hands.

Picked up the phone again. There was no answer at *Piper, Coretta,* so he moved on to *Harold & Margaret.* It rang twice. He was just about to hang up when a woman answered. She sounded like someone's grandmother.

"Hello?" she said.

Fitch paused. "Is Amanda there?"

"Yes," she said. "May I ask who's calling?"

"Um," he said. "Luke."

He moved the phone away from his ear so he could lightly smack his head with it. God, what an idiot. *Luke?* Where did that come from? Why didn't he just say his real name?

"Luke who?" the woman said.

"Luke . . ." His mind said *Skywalker*, but that

was just too ridiculous. Why was he so stupid? "Just Luke."

The woman paused. "Just a moment."

He heard the phone rattle as she put it down. Then, muffled: "Amanda! Phone!"

What was he going to say?

He'd practiced something in his head, of course, but all those words left him now.

When Amanda picked up, her voice sounded like something from his imagination. A phantom. A ghost.

"Hello?" she said.

He opened his mouth.

No words formed.

"Hello?" she said.

He swallowed.

Could she hear his heart beating through the phone?

"Uh." He mumbled something like *I'm sorry,* but it didn't sound quite as he'd intended. He wasn't sure if it even sounded like *words.*

"Hello?" Amanda said again.

Apparently, it hadn't sounded like words.

It had sounded like nothing.

Just like he felt.

He hung up.

SEND WORD TO BIRD

As far as Cash's father was concerned, there was only one battle more intense than the Cold War between the United States and the Soviet Union, and that was the rivalry between the Philadelphia 76ers and the Boston Celtics.

Tonight they'd take the court right in the Nelson Thomas living room, via channel four.

Cash and his father had anticipated the game all week. They sat in their respective places near the coffee table, which was littered with more junk food than they could ever eat. Chips and dip. Soft pretzels. Pizza rolls. Cheez Balls. Cash's mother typically spent such evenings reading in her room, but when she *did* wander in, she never failed to remark on the mountain of fat and calories they were stuffing into their faces.

"Dr. J can't find the basket tonight," his father said at the half. The Sixers were only up by one. He was acting antsy about it, sitting up straight on the edge of the couch, bouncing his feet and eating one chip after another.

"He's shooting better than Barkley," said Cash. He felt defensive when someone spoke against Julius Irving, as if they were close personal friends and he needed to defend Dr. J's honor.

"All I want is to beat Larry Bird at home," his father replied, his mouth full. "If we pound them at the Garden, I'll run down the street singing."

Cash laughed and rummaged behind the cushions for the bent coat hanger he'd been using to scratch under his cast. God, he couldn't *wait* to get this thing off.

"I'm serious," his dad said. "Mark my words."

"What song will you sing?" asked Cash.

"I'll make up something original, like . . ." His dad swallowed, stared off into an imaginary bubble in the air, and sang at the top of his lungs, bewilderingly off-key. *"Send word to Bird! You're not even good enough for third! SEND WORD TO BIRD!"* He raised his arms and sang louder and louder, as Cash laughed. But the performance didn't last long. Soon enough, Bird Nelson Thomas—not Larry—was standing in their basketball-only zone, looking quite confused.

Their father stopped singing but was still smiling. "Hey there. Want some snacks?" he asked.

Bird glanced between her father and brother. "Were you calling me?"

A moment of confusion passed between Cash and his dad.

"I heard my name," Bird explained.

"Oh!" Mr. Thomas said. "No. I mean, yes, it was your name, but I was singing about Larry Bird,

WE DREAM OF SPACE

not our Bird." He gestured toward the television.

"Oh," Bird said. "Okay, then."

She turned around and had taken two steps back toward her room before her father said, "You wanna watch the game with us?"

"No, thanks."

"You sure? No need to stay cooped up in your room like your mom and your brother."

"I know," Bird mumbled.

"Everything okay? You seem . . . I don't know. Quiet."

Before Bird could answer, Mrs. Thomas appeared down the hall with a paperback tucked under her arm and an empty water glass in her hand. She walked toward the kitchen.

"Bird's bummed out about the *Challenger* launch," said Cash. He snatched a pizza roll and popped it in his mouth. "They keep rescheduling it."

"Yeah, I was reading about that in the paper this morning," said Mr. Thomas. He leaned back and returned his attention to the television, where it was still halftime. The volume was lowered. "If you ask me, they shouldn't be going at all. Sending men and women in space together." He shook his head. "Recipe for disaster."

The faucet in the kitchen stopped running.

"What did you say?" said Mrs. Thomas. She placed her full glass on the counter.

Cash and Bird exchanged looks.

"What?" Mr. Thomas said, eyes still on the TV. "I just don't think it's a good idea, that's all. I'm entitled to my opinion."

Mrs. Thomas crossed her arms. She was standing behind the kitchen island like a general eyeing a disobedient army.

"Please enlighten me," she said.

"Look," he replied, making eye contact. "It's just not good for men and women to be in such close quarters for a long period of time like that. You get a bad mix together, and bam! Disaster. They've got two women on the *Challenger*, right? What happens if both of them get their . . . you know . . . at the same time? It's not like there's a drugstore down the street at the space station. Not to mention the mood swings and tensions. Too much can go wrong."

Mrs. Thomas raised her eyebrows. She uncrossed her arms and put her hands on her hips.

"Do you have any idea how ignorant you sound right now, in front of your children?" she said.

Mr. Thomas looked at Cash. Then at Bird. Then at the television.

"So much for *equality*," he mumbled. "You can't even disagree with a woman anymore without being accused of being a—"

"I can *hear you*, Mike. My ears *work*, you know."

Cash focused on the screen and the first-half highlights. He couldn't hear the announcers over his parents, but so what? He'd focus on what he was seeing. Here was Charles Barkley. Here was Larry Bird. Here was Dr. J.

Here was his sister, disappearing back into her room.

BENEFITS TO BEING INVISIBLE

There are some benefits to being invisible. When the house shifts to Mr. Hyde, no one pays attention to what you're doing. You can slip out the door in your winter coat, gloves, and hat, even though it's incredibly cold and icy after a day of light rain. You can even take your parent's keys with you, get into a car, and turn the ignition. You can't leave, of course—you don't know how to drive—but you can turn on the heater and look at the stars through the window.

There was Venus. The brightest object in

the night sky, second to the moon. According to Ms. Salonga, Venus was the hottest planet in the solar system. Mercury was closest to the sun, but Venus's atmosphere allowed it to reach up to eight hundred and seventy degrees. Such temperatures seemed unfathomable, especially when you were sitting in the cold night air of north Delaware.

Bird wondered where Halley's Comet was at this exact moment. What would it be like to see it up close, like the *Challenger* crew would? What would it be like to see the stars from the window of a space shuttle instead of a Cavalier?

Bird closed her eyes. She imagined that the hum of the car was the hum of solid rocket boosters. She held on to the sides of the driver's seat. But it wasn't a car's seat. It was a *shuttle* seat. Judith was next to her. This mission would decide whether or not she would be promoted to shuttle commander. Nothing could go wrong.

"All systems go," Bird said.

Then, the countdown: ten, nine, eight, seven, six, five, four, three, two—

Knock, knock, knock.

A foreign object was banging against the shuttle window.

Pay no attention. Probably just debris.

What number were we on?

—four, three, two—

KNOCK. KNOCK. WHATAREYOUDOING?

Don't open your eyes.

Don't worry, Judith. Just debris. All systems go.

AREYOUCRAZYBIRD?

The solid rocket boosters quieted. Judith disappeared—poof!—and the hum of the engine settled to an earthly buzz.

Bird opened her eyes.

Fitch was standing next to the car, giving her a bewildered look.

She rolled down the window. *Squeak, squeak, squeak.* Cold air rushed in.

"What are you doing?" he asked. He wasn't

even wearing a jacket. Just a long-sleeve Donkey Kong T-shirt. The shirt was so worn that Donkey Kong was cracked and faded. "Stealing the car or something?"

"No," Bird said. "I'm just sitting here. I turned the heater on because it's cold."

"They're done arguing," said Fitch, motioning toward the house. Puffs of cold air came out of his mouth as he spoke. "Mom went to their room, and Dad is watching the stupid game."

"Okay," Bird said.

"You can come back inside now. You don't have to stay out here."

"Maybe," said Bird.

She wanted to ask: *How did you find me? I thought I was invisible.* But she let it be.

Fitch hugged his chest. "Are you coming in?"

"Maybe."

Fitch glanced back toward the front door. "You're gonna get in trouble if Dad finds out you started the car."

"Probably."

Being in trouble was a strange thought. She'd never been in trouble before.

Bird started to roll up the window. *Squeak, squeak.* But Fitch put his hand on it before it closed completely.

"I'm gonna come in, too," he said, nodding toward the passenger seat.

Bird didn't have time to protest. She wasn't sure if she even wanted to. Instead she rolled up her window and leaned over to unlock the passenger side. Fitch got in, rubbed his hands together, and aimed the heater vents toward his face.

"It's freezing!" he said.

"You aren't wearing a jacket."

"What're you doing out here?"

Bird shrugged.

Fitch cupped his hands around his mouth and blew into them.

"Are you looking at the stars or something?" he asked. "I don't understand why you won't go in the backyard to do that. You'd probably get a better view."

"It's cold," she said.

And backyards are meant to be shared.

Backyards are meant for dogs. Barbecues. Families.

Our backyard is a lonely place.

I don't want a lonely place.

They sat together in silence until Fitch finally warmed up, put his hands in his lap, and stared out the window.

Our mission has been aborted, Judith, Bird thought.

"You know what I think is kinda cool? Black holes," Fitch said. "The way they suck in everything, like a vacuum. *Shhhooop.* But Ms. Salonga said we can't even see them. And if we can't see them, how do we know they're there?"

Bird paused. "Their gravitational pull is so strong that it consumes everything around it, including light. That's why we can't see it."

Bird put her hands on the steering wheel.

"Hey, Bird?" said Fitch. He leaned back on the headrest and turned toward her. "I'm sorry." He cleared his throat. "About what I said."

What would it be like to drive forever?

"I mean it," Fitch said. "My apology, that is."

What would it be like to drive down the interstate and never stop?

"Sometimes I say things and I don't know why," he continued.

Bird swallowed. "Maybe you were right," she said.

Fitch looked out the window again. "Me? Nah. I'm never right."

A shadow passed across the living room window.

"We should go back in before they come out," Fitch said. "You coming?"

She didn't want to, but Fitch had a point. It was time to cancel the launch for now. Sometimes all systems weren't go. She killed the engine and followed her brother into the house. Cash was putting leftover food in the refrigerator.

He looked up when they came in.

"The Sixers lost," Cash said.

"We care," Fitch replied dryly, rolling his eyes.

Bird didn't say anything. Usually she took off her coat and hung it on the hook by the front door, but tonight she kept everything on until she was in her bedroom. Then she put her jacket, hat, and gloves in a pile on the floor, turned off the lights, and fell back on her bed fully dressed. Even her shoes.

Her mind swam and swam.

She was just a girl from Delaware.

She was plain.

Girls didn't belong in space, anyway.

Besides, she was invisible.

The truth is the hardest thing to hear sometimes.

She closed her eyes.

She wanted to go to sleep for now.

She was tired.

It was time to face the truth. All of it.

She would never go into space. Who was she kidding?

She would never be a NASA shuttle commander.

She would never be Judith Resnik.

She was just a plain, plain girl, floating like dust. She didn't know Judith Resnik. They weren't even real conversations and didn't make a difference in the world. She was no better than a five-year-old with an imaginary friend.

What difference did it make if Bird talked to her or said good night or not?

None.

THIS MOMENT

Fitch wouldn't have thought it possible for two people to attend Park Middle School in the same grade and never cross paths. School was like its own mini-universe, after all. Identical stars and planets, identical orbits, floating through the same galaxy, day after day after day. But somehow, Amanda Piper had managed to elude him for weeks. Today he would find her. He would finally, *finally* make amends.

He couldn't take it anymore. The unsaid apology followed him everywhere. He wanted to swat it away. He wanted to believe that it didn't matter and he should just go on with his life. But he couldn't. He'd apologized to his sister, and now he would apologize to Amanda Piper, and then he could move on without feeling like such a failure.

When someone finally, *finally*, told him that Amanda had Ms. Salonga for sixth period, he hurried down the hall as soon as fifth period ended and lingered near the classroom door. He'd catch her on the way in.

She didn't see him at first because she was looking down as she walked. When she saw him, her eyes darted away and she took a half step in the opposite direction.

"Amanda!" he called, narrowing the distance between them.

She stopped and turned. She hugged her books close to her chest, which rounded her shoulders. She didn't look at him.

"Hey," he said. He motioned to an empty space by the lockers. "Um . . . can I talk to you for a second?"

They stepped off to the side.

Fitch's heart raced. He adjusted his backpack.

"Um . . ." he said. "I just wanted to say . . ."

He looked at the toes of his sneakers, but for whatever reason—maybe because of where they were standing, who knows—Ms. Salonga's words drifted into his consciousness. Something she always said in class when someone wasn't paying attention.

Eye contact is the simplest gift you can give someone.

Yes, something like that.

Fitch picked his head up.

"I'm sorry, Amanda," he said.

The words came out crisp and true.

He'd never said anything with so much conviction. He surprised even himself.

The words hung in the air between them.

Amanda looked up, too. For a split second, their eyes met. But that was all.

She didn't say *okay*.

She didn't say *thank you.*

She didn't say *it's fine.*

He wasn't sure what he expected, but he thought she'd say something.

She didn't.

She walked past him and into Ms. Salonga's classroom.

But the words were said. They were out there. It didn't change the past, but it certainly influenced this moment—the present.

He exhaled.

11:37 A.M. EST

Rows of chairs were set up in front of the TV. Bird had darted into the room first and took a seat in the front row, right in the center. By the time Dani and Devonte walked in, the seats around Bird were filled. She hadn't thought to save a seat for Dani. Too much excitement. She wondered absently where Dani was sitting, but she could hardly sit still long enough to look around. Plus, she didn't want to take her eyes off the television.

The launch had been rescheduled several

times, so Ms. Salonga—and Bird, for that matter— was cautiously optimistic. But it was really going to happen today. Bird could *feel* it. Her belly was doing somersaults. Everything else that had been wrong these past few weeks had dimmed in the light of this moment. The universe had tilted and become surreal. Here she was, surrounded by kids from other classes, many of whom she barely recognized, all of them sharing this moment—or the moment that was about to happen, anyway.

Bird wondered what they had written in their essays.

She was the only one who'd brought a notebook, she noticed.

"The countdown could be halted again," Ms. Salonga was saying as she tightened and jiggled the various cords that snaked out from behind the television. "If that happens, don't be too disappointed."

When the image came through fuzzy, a boy Bird didn't know hopped up to help Ms. Salonga figure it out. Bird was near panic at the thought that the picture wouldn't straighten itself out, but it did. She trained her eyes on the screen, her pen at the ready. She didn't want to miss a thing.

Someone turned out the lights. Ms. Salonga stood in the glow of the TV, where the shuttle sat on the launch pad. The astronauts were already on board. So was Bird. She could feel the weight of the helmet on her head. The push of the seat belt against her shoulders.

Her notebook bounced on her lap.

"After the launch, we'll have a quick lesson to discuss what we witnessed, and how that relates to what you've already learned so far," Ms. Salonga said. She smiled.

In the dark, the quiet whispers and glow of the television made everything surreal.

Bird heard a crackle.

A man's voice.

Mission control.

Was it really happening or in her imagination?

"We've had a go for auto-sequence start," he said. "The SRB hydraulic power units have started. T-minus twenty-one seconds and the solid rocket booster engine gimbal now underway."

Bird wrote down *gimbal* so she could look it up later, then she placed her hands on either side of her seat and held on. The engine rumbled. Preflight checks complete.

Her heart pounded in her ears. *Thrum-thrum-thrum.*

She was nervous. She had the sudden urge to jump out of her chair and leap into the television set so she could sit somewhere on that shuttle, anywhere, next to Judith, next to the pilot, in the cargo bay, even. She didn't care where.

She stared at the screen and willed it to happen.

The television was the sun in a dark, dark room, but it didn't hurt to look.

Not yet.

11:38 A.M. EST

If you traveled out of Ms. Salonga's class, into the hallway, and down four doors, you'd arrive at Mr. Wills's social studies class. The students in Mr. Wills's class were not watching the launch. They had not written essays in exchange for a seat in the auditorium. They didn't know what was happening on the television, and they certainly couldn't *hear* it. They didn't know the news announcer had reached T-minus fifteen seconds.

That was around the time Fitch dropped his pencil.

He watched it roll under Penny Barnard's desk. The lead point broke off along the way.

Someone will step on that and they won't even notice, Fitch thought. *It'll probably leave a scuff mark.*

His mind wasn't exactly bursting at top speed, but it was difficult to get your brain moving in

Mr. Wills's class. Mr. Wills spoke in a monotone and seemed ready to fall into a deep coma at any moment. Most of his lectures consisted of him reading aloud from the textbook. He rarely stood up from his desk. Sometimes he gave them "free time," wherein they were expected to dive into their social studies textbooks as he graded papers; in reality, most people passed notes, whispered back and forth, or drew crude doodles of Mr. Wills in ridiculous situations. Here is Mr. Wills flying a plane, half asleep. Here is Mr. Wills skydiving, half asleep. Here is Mr. Wills performing brain surgery, half asleep.

Fitch's eyes were trained on the pencil, as if it was putting him in a trance.

He yawned.

He looked at the clock for the five-millionth time.

Everyone looked at the clock five million times in Mr. Wills's class. Even Mr. Wills.

At eleven-fifty, the lunch bell would ring, and he would be free. For today, at least.

Fitch was thinking: *I wonder what's for lunch?* when he heard a strange noise. Everyone heard it. Mr. Wills had been droning on about the New Deal but stopped mid-sentence and turned toward the classroom door. It was a scream, maybe, or a wail. It was hard to tell.

No one moved.

Then: another sound.

WHAP!

Fitch knew that sound well—it was a door ricocheting off an opposing wall.

"What—," said Mr. Wills, striding toward the hallway. He placed his hand on the door frame and leaned out.

Something blurred past, down the hall.

No, not *something.*

Someone.

Not just someone.

Bird.

Fitch bolted out of his chair. The sudden movement startled several of his classmates. They jumped and stared at him. Everyone knew he was a hothead. Was he about to have a "moment"?

No, he was walking toward the door, saying "That was my sister!"

Fitch and Mr. Wills stood side by side, an unlikely pair, and watched Bird disappear into the girls' bathroom. Fitch had conflicting instincts all at once: one of his feet wanted to chase after Bird, the other wanted to stay put until he knew what was going on.

He listened to the second foot.

He didn't move until Mr. Wills started walking down the hall, toward the auditorium.

Fitch followed him.

Ms. Salonga was standing near the light switch. She had a strange look on her face. About a hundred kids were seated in chairs behind her, talking to each other, staring at a blank television, staring at Fitch, asking questions, shifting in their seats.

Goose bumps erupted on Fitch's arms.

Ms. Salonga's eyes were glassy.

"What happened?" Mr. Wills asked.

"The shuttle," Ms. Salonga said.

11:42 A.M. EST

English was Cash's least favorite class, which was saying a lot, considering he despised all his classes. But he was determined to raise his grade-point average by any means necessary. In this case, that meant he had to come up with sentences that used all their vocabulary words. He needed ten of them before the lunch bell rang, and thus far, he only had seven. Most of the class was already finished; their papers were facedown. He never understood how people got their work done so quickly. In the past, he would have rushed through it, written anything, just so he wouldn't be last. Not today. Today he was determined.

He tapped his pencil on his paper. He stared at the word *melancholy*.

Melancholy. Melancholy. Melancholy.

Oh, yes. He remembered what that meant.

He had three words of his sentence using *melancholy* when someone knocked on the classroom door. Whoever it was didn't wait. The door opened. It was Mr. Wills. He was frowning.

The English teacher, Ms. Pachenko, stood at her desk and raised her eyebrows at him.

"Yes?" she said.

Mr. Wills blurted it out in three, quick words. "The shuttle exploded."

"The shuttle?" said Ms. Pachenko.

"The *Challenger*. It exploded."

"How can something explode in space?" asked some kid who sat behind Cash.

"It didn't explode in space," said Mr. Wills. He was still looking at Ms. Pachenko. "It exploded right after it took off. It never made it."

It never made it.

Cash looked down at his vocabulary words again.

He felt an emotion he couldn't explain.

The other kids were talking. Someone even laughed. Made a joke.

What was funny about a shuttle exploding?

The class spoke in whispers at first, then in normal tones, as Mr. Wills told Ms. Pachenko the few details that he knew.

"Bird," said Cash, to no one but himself.

LUNCH

Bird's legs hurt. She'd been standing in the bathroom stall for a long time. She wasn't sure how long. She'd darted out of the auditorium not long after the malfunction. That's how she was framing it in her mind: a malfunction. *Explosion* didn't seem possible. *Malfunction* felt safer, more comfortable. People survived malfunctions. Besides, that's what the guy from mission control had said. *Obviously a major malfunction,* he'd said. And he didn't sound panicked, so maybe there was nothing to panic over. People panicked over explosions. They didn't panic over malfunctions.

That's what she'd been telling herself.

But the truth was the hardest thing to hear sometimes.

And the truth was, she'd escaped into a bathroom stall because it was more than a simple malfunction, and she knew that. She knew machines. And she wasn't an astronaut, but she knew *this* machine, the space shuttle *Challenger*. And she knew that it wasn't supposed to break apart that way. As soon as the major malfunction happened, someone said, "Is that supposed to happen, Ms. Salonga?" but Ms. Salonga didn't answer because she had her hand over her mouth. But Bird knew: No, of course not. That's not supposed to happen.

No one said anything. Or maybe people said things, but Bird couldn't hear them. Her ears were flooded with the sound of her heart. She stared at the columns of smoke branching off in every direction and desperately wished mission control would say something, anything, either on TV or into her nonexistent helmet. She waited for the shuttle to emerge through the plume and continue on its way. She waited for Judith to speak.

She felt sick.

After the words "major malfunction," Ms. Salonga turned to them with a strange look in her eyes, like she'd forgotten they were there or what she was doing. Then she rushed to turn off the television with shaky hands. She didn't know what to say, that much was clear. She just stood there, frozen.

That's when Bird took off.

Her notebook fell from her lap to the floor.

She thought she was going to throw up.

She went into a stall, leaned over the toilet, but nothing happened.

She stood up. Leaned against one of the walls. There was no cover on the toilet seat, so she couldn't sit down. But she didn't want to go back to that room. That's where the television was. That's where the major malfunction happened. That's where her teacher was standing, dazed and confused.

Everyone had seen her run out, but no one had come to look for her.

That was fine.

She needed to be alone, anyway.

One of the benefits to being invisible.

When the bell rang for the next period, she was still standing there. She'd missed lunch, but so what? She wasn't even hungry. Girls shook the handle on the door, then saw her feet and used another stall. Bird maneuvered herself between the toilet and the corner and was able to relax her knees a little. She listened to girls talk about nothing and giggle over nothing. How could anyone think about anything else? The shuttle, the shuttle, the shuttle. It ran through her mind on a loop. All that smoke curling off like devilish fingers against a bright, blue sky.

Then finally: someone mentioned it. Mr. Crowe, the principal, made an announcement over the PSA.

After lunch, students would be dismissed for the rest of the day.

". . . to mourn the loss of the space shuttle *Challenger*," Mr. Crowe said.

The girls in the bathroom clapped. They remarked on their good luck. School was out for the rest of the day! It was like finding a ten-dollar bill in your pocket that you didn't know was there. They were *happy*.

Bird felt sick again. She put her hands over her ears.

How could they clap? How could they be happy?

No, this was all wrong.

They were supposed to be going to space.

They were supposed to be going to space.

A DIFFERENT SPACE

You wouldn't have guessed that there had been a national tragedy. Most kids were giddy in the seventh-grade hallway, brimming with possibility at their day off. Fitch had a feeling Vern would be one of them, so when he saw him down the hall, lingering near Fitch's locker, waiting—no doubt— for their inevitable trip to the arcade on Main, Fitch ducked out of the way. He'd wait until Vern lost patience and left. He couldn't handle Vern right now—not his voice or his chattering or his excitement. Fitch felt no levels of excitement. All he could think about was Bird.

Vern craned his neck, looking. Fitch turned toward the wall, mostly hidden behind a bank of lockers, and discovered he was looking directly at the nose of the *Challenger*, taped to the wall. He was in front of Ms. Salonga's classroom. The door was closed and the lights were off, but sunlight filled the room anyway and he saw Ms. Salonga sitting at her desk. She wasn't doing anything. Just sitting.

Fitch's heart skipped. He felt like he was seeing something he wasn't supposed to see, but he didn't want to walk away. He knocked lightly, but Ms. Salonga didn't respond. He knocked again. When she turned toward the door without getting up, he slipped inside, trying to be as inconspicuous as possible so none of the other kids noticed.

They didn't.

They were too busy embracing their freedom.

Fitch stepped inside and closed the door. He'd

been in this classroom a hundred times, but it seemed like a completely different space now. The desks were empty. Ms. Salonga wasn't at the board, tossing chalk and putting them into groups. She smiled at him faintly, but still didn't get up.

"Hi, Fitch," she said. "Did you need something?"

Her eyes were tired. Maybe she'd been crying, but she wasn't now. There was something unnatural about watching a grown-up cry right in front of you. He hoped, with every molecule in his body, that she wouldn't. What would he do if she did?

He shoved his hands in his pockets without stepping further into the room. He wasn't sure what he was doing, exactly.

He never knew.

"No. I just . . ." Fitch stammered. Sounds from the hallway drifted in. Someone was laughing, loudly. It pierced through the silent classroom. "Uh. I don't know. I guess I wanted to ask if you were okay?"

He discovered now that this was the truth.

Yes, *this* was why he'd walked in.

He wanted to check in on his teacher.

Imagine that.

"No, but I will be," Ms. Salonga said. "Don't worry about me. Just keep an eye on your sister. Okay?"

Fitch nodded.

A lump had formed in his throat, though he didn't know why or when.

"Okay," he said.

HOME

Cash and Fitch were waiting for her at the front doors. This was further evidence that the day was abnormal. In all the years they'd gone to school, her brothers had never waited for her unless one of their parents made them. Yet, here they were, standing side by side, looking for her.

They didn't look happy that school was out for the rest of the day.

In fact, they didn't look happy at all.

"I'm sorry, Bird," Fitch said, as soon as she came into view.

"Yeah," said Cash. "Me, too."

They fell in step, the three of them.

They had never fallen in step before.

But Bird didn't have time to consider what this meant, if anything.

What did it feel like when the engines turned on? Were the astronauts holding on tight? Did they feel the rumble in their chests? Was Judith smiling? What did it feel like to have a "major malfunction"?

Machines were supposed to be reliable.

Machines were supposed to do what humans told them to do.

Machines weren't supposed to make mistakes.

Mistakes were for humans. Not machines.

Bird looked at her feet as she walked. Her brothers stayed with her, even though she was moving slowly. She wanted to look at the sky to see if she'd see anything—anything at all—but she was afraid, so she didn't. She kept her eyes down.

They walked in silence all the way home.

Fitch got the key out of the mailbox. Once they were inside and had their jackets on pegs, Fitch went into the kitchen and asked Bird if she wanted a sandwich. She didn't answer, so he made one anyway. Peanut butter and jelly.

Cash turned on the television. They were showing footage from the explosion. Part of Bird wanted to watch it—Maybe there was a mistake? Maybe she dreamed the entire thing?—but another part of her didn't want to see anything.

Ultimately, it didn't matter. Cash turned it off.

"I don't feel like watching TV," he said.

But that wasn't true.

Cash *always* felt like watching TV.

Bird didn't say anything. Her mind struggled to understand this strange new world.

If she and her siblings were a machine, she would call quality control. Things were out of the ordinary. The machine wasn't working right.

Since when did her brothers care?

Since when did anyone?

TICK TICK

When Bird took the key out of the magnetic door knocker at Dani Logan's house, she acted casual, as if this were an everyday occurrence. Blood rushed her ears. Her heart beat all the way up to her throat. She half expected a wail of sirens to blare as soon as she put the key in the lock, but it turned easily. The door opened easily. She stepped in easily.

Everything that happened at Dani Logan's house happened easily.

It was nine o'clock in the morning, and no one

was home. The Logans were at work, presumably, and Dani had gone to school. Bird had not. She'd spent the previous afternoon, evening, and night in her room, although she wasn't sure exactly how she'd passed the hours. She emerged to eat dinner—everyone in their separate quarters, as usual—and said a few obligatory words to her parents, but mostly she stayed tucked away, on her bed, curled up in her pajamas. The TV seemed to play nothing but footage from the disaster, comments from experts, statements from politicians. Bird heard the muffled sounds of it all through her door. Once she went into the kitchen to get a glass of water, and caught her dad mid-sentence, ". . . teachers aren't real astronauts, so it doesn't make sense that NASA would . . ."

She thought of Ms. Salonga.

She didn't wait for the rest of the sentence.

In the morning—just hours before she found herself here, on the Logans' doorstep—she told her parents she didn't feel well and they said she could stay home. It was easy for Bird to get a pass from her parents. She never did anything wrong; why would they worry?

Once inside the Logans' house, she took off her shoes and set them aside. Those were the rules, after all. Her feet were cold. She rubbed one socked foot on top of the other while she stood there.

"I'm home!" she called out, even though she knew no one was there.

It had taken more than half an hour to walk to Dani's house. Bird's nose was red and her hands were cold, even though she'd worn her gloves. She slipped the house key into her pocket, then took off all her winter gear. The Logans had a front hall closet just for coats. They hung there obediently and neatly. Bird put hers in there, too.

The Logan house was warm.

Bird took one step forward. Two. Soon she was in the living room. She eyed the coffee table where she and Dani had spread out their junk food and drunk soda. She walked to the kitchen. Opened the refrigerator. Removed a Sunkist. When she opened the can, the *chhh* of escaped carbonation filled the emptiness. She stood by one of the kitchen counters and took a deep sip. She put the soda on a coaster.

The Logans had a kitchen island in their house, but it was nothing like the one at the Nelson Thomases'. The Logans' kitchen island was marbled, and polished. The Logans' house had two stories, not one. A set of oak stairs led to the second floor. A set of carpeted stairs led down to the basement. There was ample space here. Space to breathe, move, exist.

Bird leaned over the fancy island and faced the two empty barstools on the other side.

"Things didn't go as expected yesterday," she said.

A clock ticked somewhere.

Bird hadn't noticed that before.

It had never been so quiet anywhere on Earth.

Tick.

Tick.

Tick.

She straightened up and walked into the adjoining dining room.

She sat in the same chair as before.

Tick.

Tick.

Tick.

How long did she sit there? She couldn't be sure. But she must have been sitting still—she must have been sitting *very* still—because something moved in her peripheral vision and she knew right away what it was. She didn't move her head. Only her eyes.

Yes.

Chekov.

He was slender. Most of his fur was sleek and black, but his underbelly was white, just like the tip of his tail, which swung lazily in the air behind him. He stepped cautiously, one paw in front of the other. Bird was afraid to move. She didn't want to scare him.

He paused when he saw her. Stopped.

Bird turned her head, slowly, slowly.

Chekov stepped forward. One step, two.

He meowed.

"It's okay," Bird whispered.

He seemed to understand.

He closed the distance between them quickly. Rubbed against her shins. Wove in and out.

When he meowed again and put his paws on the edge of the chair, Bird took a chance and lifted him up. He didn't mind. He nuzzled and purred.

She scratched his back.

She put her nose in his fur.

"They didn't make it," she said.

At some point Bird fell asleep on the couch, and when she woke up, Chekov was nowhere to be seen. For a moment she forgot where she was. She breathed in the fresh scent of the throw pillow. She looked at the clean white ceiling above her. She turned to the mantel, where a clock ticked methodically.

And then she remembered.

It was past noon. She'd slept for a long time, and her body ached.

She sat up, stretched, and yawned.

She called for Chekov, but he didn't come.

She finished her soda and placed it carefully in the trash.

She turned on the television. *Days of Our Lives* was on, which made her think of her mother.

She wondered if Mrs. Logan ever watched soap operas.

She wished she could stay here, on this couch, forever.

She wished the Logans would come home, see her there, and act like it was totally normal. *We'll show you to your room,* they would say. They would make dinner together and sit at the table and do cheers at her good ideas, whatever they were. After they set their glasses down, she would ask, "Is it okay to cry for people you don't know?" And they would comfort her. They would hear, really hear, every word she said. They would sit on either side of her and nothing would be about them. No raised voices. No lost questions. Just *consensus*.

She wished she was part of a different family.

She wished she was part of *this* family.

It wasn't a pretty thought.

But there it was.

THAT NIGHT

Bird: I'm sorry.

Bird:

Bird:

Bird:

Bird:

Bird:

Bird:

Bird:

Bird:

Bird:

FIRST PERIOD

Fitch never thought of his family as a machine. His mind wasn't built like Bird's. When he thought of his family, he thought of sounds. His parents shouting. Music from his boom box. Basketball on the television and his brother and father hooting and hollering about things he wasn't a part of; sports he didn't understand. And he thought of his mother, her disappointed voice, her huffs and sighs.

But he never thought about Bird.

Not really.

Not until now.

She'd stayed home from school again today. Ms. Salonga had come to school after a full day's absence, but Bird mumbled that she still didn't feel well and their parents didn't push the issue.

He'd never noticed before how each sound in the house affected the others, including Bird's silence. She wasn't loud to begin with, but her quietness had become the loudest thing in the family. Last night he'd knocked on her door to ask if she was okay. At one point Cash had casually asked if she had any new schematics. That's when Fitch realized that no one had ever really asked about Bird's drawings before. She went to her room without answering; he wasn't even sure she'd heard them.

Fitch was rolling all these thoughts over in his head when Ms. Salonga started class.

Her eyes still looked tired.

When the tardy bell rang, she stood in front of her desk and leaned against it. She looked at all of them and none of them at once. She brought her hands together, put them under her chin, then dropped them at her sides.

"Class," she began. "I want to talk about what happened on Tuesday. We spent the entire month preparing for this launch, and . . . well, obviously it didn't go as planned." Inhale. "As you know, the *Challenger* meant a lot to me. I know it meant a lot to you, too. And even though many of you would never admit it, I'm sure there are people in this room who are going through a mix of emotions. I know I am. Sadness and confusion, mostly. I want to know what went wrong, and why. Mostly I'm thinking about the astronauts. I'm thinking about all the opportunities they'll miss, and the ones we'll miss, too. There are many people out there who are angry and believe this was all for nothing. They say we should end the space program before more lives and money are lost. And that worries me, too." Pause. "Last week, I asked each of your crews to come up with five reasons why we should invest in space exploration. Some of you struggled with this question. Many of you said you couldn't come up with one reason. Many of you asked—that day and other days—*What's the point, Ms. Salonga? We're this one little planet in this huge universe. How could we ever begin to know what's out there? It's too big, too vast.* I have an answer for you—"

SECOND PERIOD

"—And it's pretty simple, really. The only way for us to know what's out there is if we're out there, too. Yes, we are small. Yes, there are things we may never understand. But to be small is not to be inconsequential. Never mistake size for might."

Ms. Salonga paced the front of the room, like her thoughts were floating in the air and she needed to catch up to them.

Some of the students rolled their eyes,

exasperated at any lecture, trying to *act casual* and pretend they didn't care. But Cash cared. At that moment, he cared a great deal.

Things had shifted at home since Tuesday. There was a mood over the Nelson Thomas house. There was always a mood over the house, to be honest, but not this kind. At first he thought it was everywhere, as if the tragedy had blanketed American neighborhoods with a sense of surreal melancholy. But it *wasn't* everywhere. The school hallways weren't much different. Brant and Kenny were their same selves. Everyone seemed to be doing what they always did.

Last night, as he stared at Dr. J, wondering if Dr. J had seen the shuttle explosion and wondering what he thought about it, Cash realized that the tone of the house had been set by Bird. Not on purpose. It just was. Bird was the even-tempered rock of the family. She didn't lose her temper like Fitch. She didn't yell and argue like their parents. She didn't break bones or flunk out. She was just Bird.

Cash thought about the night she'd told him how many days there were in summer vacation.

He thought of how she offered to bring him his homework after he broke his wrist.

He thought of how she'd tagged along to the X-ray room to ask a million questions.

He thought of other things, too.

Like all those schematics he knew nothing about. And the time she tried to talk to him about space and he was frozen by Mumm-Ra.

He wondered: What's she doing now?

"Did you know that removing one single grain of sand can change an entire beach? A *single grain of sand*. Earth may be a tiny pinprick in comparison with the whole universe, but that doesn't make it any more or less impactful than the sun or the moon." Ms. Salonga was back at her desk again. She leaned on the corner. "If the sand never moves, it never changes. And each of us should strive to change every single day. To be better explorers.

To be better teachers and students. To be better humans. To just *be better*." She paused. She seemed to look directly at Cash, but maybe it was his imagination. "The astronauts on the *Challenger* trained rigorously for months to become the best explorers this nation had to offer, despite the risks, despite the possibility that the worst would happen. We owe it to ourselves, and to everyone, to offer our best to the world. To quote the words of one of the brightest people I know: The universe is waiting. So what are *we* waiting for?"

BRIGHT STAR

Checking the pay phone for forgotten quarters had become rote for Fitch and Vern. One of them would inevitably break away from the sidewalk on their way to the arcade and beeline to the dingy phone on the side of the gas station. After a quick swipe through the coin return—yielding nothing, always—the journey would continue.

Today it was Fitch who jogged over.

Today it was Fitch who swiped the coin return.

Today he found a quarter.

His fingertips brushed its familiar ridged edges.

His ears heard the clink of the coin.

It was like finding gold.

ONE OF BILLIONS

Bird gathered all her schematics. She held them in her arms, close to her chest, and stood up from her desk. She walked into the kitchen.

There were more than she'd thought. When she first put them in a pile, a twinge of pride moved through her, and she quickly stamped it down. She slipped her pride underneath a steel compressor and bore down until it flattened out and disappeared.

The compressor was called reality.

She was plain.

She was just a girl.

She was just a girl in Park, Delaware.

Machines weren't worth studying.

Machines were dangerous.

She would never be an astronaut.

She shouldn't *want* to be one, anyway.

Astronauts died.

They died for nothing—because what was the point?

She was just one of billions of people, floating out in space, so small and pointless.

NEW CASH

Runners needed a healthy diet. That was true of all athletes, of course, but Cash hadn't considered himself an athlete in a long time. Today, though? Today, he was a runner in training, so when he got home from school, with no one there but Bird, he put two oranges and one banana on the counter in front of him and proceeded to eat. No junk food. This would be the start of a new life. The life of a runner. He could practically feel the wind against his face already. He was so lost in the imaginings of it all that he barely remembered eating the fruit, but suddenly he was standing there with a full belly and a pile of peels. It had been tricky to peel the fruit with his cast, but he persevered. That's what new Cash did—he persevered.

He tried to carry all of the peels in one hand to the trash, but a few wayward pieces of orange rind fell to the floor. He cursed as he opened the lid of the garbage can and tossed everything inside.

He knew something was off immediately.

A stack of papers was stuffed in the trash.

He brushed some of the peels aside, but he already knew what they were. He recognized Bird's handwriting. He saw pencil lines and arrows pointing to this and that. He picked up one peel after another—a strange reversal—and soon he was holding the peels in his hand again.

She hadn't just tossed one out.

It was an entire *stack*.

Normally he wouldn't rush to pull things out of the garbage, but he didn't think twice about it today. He tossed his peels in the sink—something to worry about later—and took the schematics out of the trash. Some of the edges were damp. Others were dotted with old coffee. For the most part, though, they were in good shape. Maybe they hadn't been in there long. He held them as best as he could in the crook of his left arm, then walked down the hall and knocked on Bird's door.

"What," she said, sounding more like Fitch than herself.

Cash had to do some fancy maneuvering to open the door without dropping all the papers, but he managed it.

Bird was sitting on her bedroom floor. She had their dad's old Walkman on her lap. The headphones draped around her neck. He couldn't tell if there was a tape inside.

"I found these in the trash," Cash said.

"So?"

"Why are you throwing them away?"

"Why not?"

"It's all your work."

"I know what they are. I'm the one who made them."

Cash's heart did something strange then. It grew and pushed against his rib cage, like a balloon filling with water.

"What's the matter with you?" Cash asked.

"Nothing," Bird said. "I'm just done with those

stupid schematics. It was a waste of time."

Cash paused. "Is this because of the *Challenger*?"

"What do you care?" said Bird. She turned her attention to the Walkman.

"Ms. Salonga talked about it today. She said a lot of stuff about how we should be our best selves because that's what the astronauts did . . ."

"Lot of good that did them, huh?"

". . . and she said something really cool about sand. Like, we're all grains of sand, and even though Earth is so small, that doesn't mean we aren't powerful, or something."

"Wow," Bird said, flatly. "Fascinating."

Cash sighed. "I'm not saying it right."

"It doesn't matter, anyway," Bird said. "I don't want my drawings, so you can put them back in the trash."

She didn't wait for him to say anything else.

She put the headphones on and turned the other way.

THE MOST PREDICTABLE MACHINE

Bird was curious about Ms. Salonga's lecture—she couldn't help herself. What had she said? Did she mention Judith Resnik? What did she say, *exactly*?—but she put her curiosity under the steel compressor. Most of all she wondered if Ms. Salonga thought people should end space exploration for good.

No. That was impossible.

Well, maybe it was impossible for Ms. Salonga, but not for Bird.

Bird was operating in reality now, and in

this new place, nothing much mattered. Judith Resnik and the other astronauts were gone forever, and they didn't make it to space. NASA had designed, studied, and built the machines, and the machines had betrayed them.

Bird spent the day molding and shaping this new belief system. When Monday came around, she was going to be a different person. She wouldn't concern herself with silly drawings or becoming the first female shuttle commander. She would direct all that energy toward things that actually mattered. Maybe she'd dust her eyelids with blue shadow like the Jessicas and figure out what she was really supposed to be doing in the world.

She didn't say a word in science. Not to Devonte, not to Ms. Salonga. She even shuffled away when Dani asked if she was okay, partly because she felt a detached sense of guilt for sneaking into Dani's house, which was technically a crime—*but this is the new me,* she told herself, *new reality, new me*—and partly because she didn't want to talk about whether she was okay or not.

Here was the plan:

She would burrow into her brain.

She would reconstruct her thoughts.

She would emerge when it was safe, like Chekov.

When she emerged, it would be a new, safer world.

It would be safer because she wouldn't have any expectations.

If you have no expectations, you have no disappointments.

She would expect nothing from herself and nothing from anyone else.

And if she didn't become a shuttle commander or whatever, it wouldn't matter, because who cared anyway?

It would just take a little mental training, that's all.

When she studied the logic under her mental microscope, she couldn't find a single flaw.

If she'd never been looking forward to the launch, then she wouldn't have had to hide in the bathroom.

If she didn't expect to be an astronaut, then it wouldn't matter if she became one or not.

Look where expectation has gotten me, she thought, as she walked home. *Wandering around other people's houses like a maniac.*

As she hung up her winter coat and tossed her backpack aside, she thought: *I wanted to be part of another family, but the reality is,* this *is my family. And families don't change. You can't count on families, just like you can't count on machines.*

As she walked into her bedroom and sat on her floor: *family is the most predictable machine of all.*

Cash was right. Or Ms. Salonga. Whoever.

We're all just grains of sand.

● ● ●

The mental gymnastics had exhausted Bird and lulled her to a deep, deep sleep. She dreamed that she was sitting with Judith on a beach. Judith was wearing her NASA coveralls.

"Good night, Bird," Judith said. She smiled. She had a dimple, just like Bird.

"It's not dark yet," Bird replied.

"I know," Judith said.

They stared out at the water, but there wasn't any water. Just sand, as far as the eye could see. A light wind blew and tickled Bird's cheek.

"Bird?" Judith said, even though her mouth wasn't moving.

Bird didn't answer.

"Bird?" Judith said again.

Bird tried to brush the sand away, but it kept tickling her.

"Bird?"

Bird's eyes fluttered. They felt so heavy.

"Bird?"

No, it wasn't Judith.

It was Fitch.

And it wasn't sand.

It was a strand of her hair, brushing her cheek.

Bird opened her eyes.

She'd fallen asleep on her bedroom floor, still in her school clothes, and Fitch was kneeling next to her. His face looked strangely soft.

Was she still dreaming?

"Dinner's ready," Fitch said. He had her winter coat slung over his arm. "Come on."

Was she dreaming?

Bird blinked and blinked and blinked.

She sat up. She felt like she'd been asleep for a hundred years. The dream had been so real, she could practically feel the sand.

But, no. She wasn't on a beach with Judith Resnik.

She was at her house.

Same old house. Same old day. Same old family.

"Dad ordered pizza," Fitch said. He held up her coat. He was wearing his already. "Put this on."

"Why?"

"Just put it on."

She slipped into her jacket and followed him, yawning, her head and spirit heavy. She wasn't even hungry, really. She didn't want pizza, but there it was, in the kitchen.

Mr. Thomas was in the living room, eating and watching *Knight Rider.*

Mrs. Thomas was at the kitchen island, picking at a salad and reading.

Neither of them looked up.

Cash was standing between the table and the sliding glass doors. He was wearing *his* coat, too, with a roll of paper towels tucked under one arm and a binder under the other.

Fitch closed the pizza box and lifted it.

"What's going on?" asked Bird. Her shoulders hurt from sleeping on the floor.

"We're gonna eat in the backyard," Fitch said

to Bird, then louder, to their parents. Cash slid open the door.

Cold air rushed into the warm house.

"Why?" Mrs. Thomas said.

"Because," Cash answered.

Bird followed her brothers outside and closed the door behind her.

NOT TODAY

Cash: So how does this work?

Fitch: How does what work?

Cash: Eating dinner together.

Fitch: I don't know. Bird's the expert.

Bird: This isn't exactly a table. We're sitting on a blanket outside in the cold.

Cash: Think of it as a grass table.

Fitch: Aren't you gonna eat, Bird?

Bird: I don't know. I'm not hungry. . . . What's that black binder?

Cash: This? Oh. Here, take it. I don't want to get grease on the cover.

Bird: . . .

Cash: What do you think of it?

Bird: Why did you do this?

Cash: I couldn't put them back in the trash. It just felt wrong. Some of them are stained, but most of them are okay. Some of the pages are crinkled, but—you want to keep them, don't you?

Bird: I guess.

Fitch: You guess?

Bird: Well. I've been thinking that maybe being a shuttle commander is a stupid idea.

Cash: What makes you think that? Because of what happened? You can't let that scare you.

Bird: I'm not scared. It just seems pointless. I mean. I don't know. I'm just a girl from Park, Delaware.

Cash: Everyone is from somewhere.

Fitch: Judith Resnik's hometown is Akron, Ohio. That's not a big fancy place. At least I don't think it is.

Bird: How do you know where Judith Resnik's from?

Fitch: The news, I guess. I must have picked it up somewhere and remembered it.

Bird: Why are you two doing all this, anyway? Putting my schematics in binders and having a winter picnic outside—it's, I don't know. Is this because you feel sorry for me or something?

Fitch: You always talk about eating dinner together, so we thought, *yeah, let's do that.*

Bird: I don't *always* talk about it. And I don't want some pity dinner, anyway.

Cash: He didn't mean it like that.

Fitch: Aren't you going to eat, Bird?

Bird: Besides, we're not eating dinner as a family. Half the family is inside.

Cash: That's the best part about the grass table, no matter how cold it is.

Fitch: They'd only ruin it.

Cash: Maybe we'll invite them to dinner someday.

Fitch: But not today.

Cash: Not today.

Bird: Not today.

MAGIC

Fitch had a found quarter and a new outlook. The world had shifted under his feet, and he wasn't sure how or when. The tightened bolts were still there, but he could move with them, loosen them. He walked into the arcade on Main, intending to channel all this positive energy into defeating the Vaxxian Empire. And just his luck: the place was virtually empty.

The quarter even *looked* like magic. Shiny, new. The date stamp was 1985. He held it in the palm of his hand and studied it for a moment before reaching down to dunk the coin inside the slot. The quarter was almost down when Fitch's eyes landed on a familiar face. Marsh. He was sitting at the Pop-A-Shot. He wasn't playing, though. The game wasn't running; all the balls were still in the carriage. He had a yo-yo that he couldn't control. Fitch watched him drop it, roll it back up, drop it, roll it back up. After several failed attempts, he pushed his glasses up his nose and sat there, tossing the yo-yo absently from one small hand to the other.

You can't even make one basket, and you think you can play this? Get serious, Marsha.

Fitch felt that descending fog again when he thought about what he'd said.

But he didn't want to feel that way. Heavy. Tight.

He thought: *Just play your game. Who cares about some stupid kid? If he can't take it, that's his fault. The Vaxxian Empire awaits.*

His feet didn't listen, though. They took one step in front of the other.

Marsh looked up when Fitch approached. His glasses had already slid halfway down his nose.

Fitch showed him the quarter.

"Have you ever played pinball?" Fitch asked.

BIRD'S ESSAY

One day, I will become NASA's first female shuttle commander. The launch of the *Challenger* will be my first real experience as an astronaut.

I'm not an astronaut, of course. Not yet. But I've listened in every class, and I don't think there's anyone in the world who is more excited about the launch than me. Well, maybe Christa McAuliffe, Judith Resnik, Dick Scobee, Ronald McNair, Ellison Onizuka, Gregory Jarvis, and Michael J. Smith. (See, I even know all their names by heart!) I won't be able to go into space with them to learn about Halley's Comet, but the least I can do is cheer them along the way. I don't want to miss *anything*.

Sometimes I look up at the sky and I see all those stars and my mind works overtime. There is so much up there to explore. Who knows what's happening in all that space? Maybe there's someone on the other side of the Milky Way, looking up the sky just like I am. Maybe they see a dot in the sky and they make a wish on it, and the dot in the sky is Earth, and they're actually wishing on *me*.

The only way to find the answer is if we go out there. It might be scary. We might not find anything. And I know it costs a lot of money, but it's worth it. We can't just settle for what's easy, or we would never discover anything.

When I stare up at the sky and see all that space, it feels like the universe is asking me to go up there. It's sending *me* an astrogram, and the astrogram says: *We're waiting for you, Bird.*

Can you imagine that? The universe is waiting. Even though I'm just a tiny grain of sand, it's waiting for *me*.

I'm ready.

ABOUT THE
CHALLENGER DISASTER

The space shuttle *Challenger* disintegrated over the Atlantic Ocean on January 28, 1986. The malfunction was caused by the failure of O-ring seals on one of the shuttle's solid rocket boosters (SRB). The O-rings were supposed to prevent pressurized burning gas from escaping the SRB, but they didn't seal properly because of cold weather during the launch. As the shuttle ascended, a plume of exhaust leaked out, and the external fuel tank ruptured. Seventy-three seconds after liftoff, the *Challenger* was torn apart.

Relatively few people watched the launch live that day. Most adults were at work, social media didn't exist, and cable news was a novelty. There was one unfortunate exception, however: American schoolchildren. NASA arranged satellite broadcasts onto TV sets in many U.S. schools so students could watch Christa McAuliffe become the first teacher in space.

Christa McAuliffe, a social studies teacher in Concord, New Hampshire, had been selected from more than 11,000 applicants. She was one of seven people who died on the *Challenger* that day. The other crew members were Shuttle Commander Francis R. Scobee, a former fighter pilot who decorated his room with model airplanes as a boy; Pilot Michael J. Smith, who had never been to space before but already wanted to go again; Mission Specialist Ronald McNair, a physicist who played the saxophone; Mission Specialist Ellison Onizuka, an Eagle Scout who loved to share macadamia nuts from his home state of Hawaii; Payload Specialist Gregory Jarvis, an electrical engineer who had been bumped from two previous missions and, like Smith, was anxious for his first trip; and, of course, Mission Specialist Judith Resnik.

As a little girl, Judith Resnik was very close to her father, who had taught her how to repair electronics and build simple machines. Judith Resnik was smart and high-achieving from an early age, but she was also a typical tween. She had two best friends, Barbara and Pam. She read all the Nancy Drew books. And she often struggled with her curly hair.

In many ways, however, she was atypical. By the time she was a teenager, she'd become a skilled classical pianist and excelled in science and math. In the Akron, Ohio, Firestone High School 1966 yearbook, there is a photo of the math club—fourteen boys, and Judy. She was the school valedictorian and went on to earn her doctorate in electrical engineering from the University of Maryland.

Judith Resnik attracted some media attention early in her career because she was one of the first female astronauts at NASA. She didn't enjoy being in the spotlight, but she was gracious.

In an April 1981 interview on the *Today* Show, journalist Tom Brokaw asked: "What's the best thing about being an astronaut?"

"Everything," she replied.

Brokaw also asked if people in her life— particularly men—were threatened by the fact that she was a female astronaut.

"If they are, they're probably not my friends," she said.

The *Challenger* mission would have been Judith Resnik's second trip to space. She'd been a mission specialist on the maiden voyage of *Discovery* on August 30, 1984. Soon after *Discovery* entered orbit, her voice came through the shuttle radio.

"The Earth looks great," she said.

She also held up a handwritten note for the closed-circuit cameras on board.

The note said: "Hi, Dad."

Eileen Collins, a graduate of Stanford University and former Air Force colonel, became NASA's first female shuttle commander in 1999. Like Bird, Eileen Collins knew she wanted to be an astronaut at an early age, but she didn't tell anyone because it seemed impossible. NASA didn't allow women into the program at that time. Even though she kept her dream a secret, that didn't mean she gave up. She joined the Air Force and was one of the first women to go through pilot training. Of the 450 pilots on the base, only 4 were women.

Eileen Collins became an astronaut in 1991 and served as a pilot or commander on four spaceflights before she retired in 2006.

In an interview with *Time*, Collins said: "I

advise others to take on challenges, even if you think they are too hard, even if you think you might fail. Give yourself challenges that are exciting, and be available to help others. There is no better feeling than helping someone else."

Bird would have been twenty-five years old—earning an advanced degree in engineering, perhaps—when Eileen Collins became shuttle commander for *Columbia* in 1999.

TO LEARN MORE:

"*Challenger*: The Shuttle Disaster That Changed NASA," Space.com

Challenger STS 51-L Accident January 28, 1986— NASA History, https://history.nasa.gov/sts_51l_challenger.html

Joanne Bernstein, Rose Blue, and Alan Jay Gerber, *Judith Resnik:* Challenger *Astronaut* (New York: Lodestar Books/Dutton, 1990)

NASA Astronauts, https://www.nasa.gov/astronauts

"Remembering Space Shuttle *Challenger*," https://www.nasa.gov/multimedia

The Astronauts Memorial Foundation, www.amfcse.org